PRANKS AND POISON

A MIRA MICHAELS MYSTERY

JULIA KOTY

BUSSTOP PRESS

Copyright © 2021 by Julia Koty

First paperback edition May 2021

Cover design by Kim Thurlow
Book design by Natasha Sass

ISBN 978-1-939309-06-8 (paperback)
ISBN 978-1-939309-07-5 (large print paperback)
ISBN 978-1- 939309-05-1(ebook)
www.JuliaKoty.com

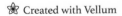

To my children Ana and Ryan,
and to my husband Joe

Also to my kitties Arnold, Rissa, Charlie and Lucy, who make
life cozy

ALSO BY JULIA KOTY

1
_____

The onions were beginning to burn again. The house already smelled like scorched vegetables. The trash can was filled with them. Arnold had abandoned me for the other room. Even Ozzy my friendly foster dog was nowhere to be found, her sensitive nose had lost tolerance as well. I couldn't seem to figure out the sauté function on this electric pressure cooker.

If I had a regular stove this wouldn't be happening, but I ignored the burned-out hole that had been my kitchen. Doing that allowed me to ignore the memory of finding the body of my realtor on my first day in town and the memory of the night of the fire when Arnold and the resident ghost, Clara, helped me get out in time.

I stirred the onions and prodded the sauté button again. Oh, it worked. The pot stopped smoking and settled into a sizzle.

I rummaged through the grocery bags I had recently brought in and found the treats I had bought for both my companions. "Hey, guys, I've got treats for you." Nothing happened. I shook the box of dog treats and the bag of kitty treats. A mini stampede of animals arrived. Ozzy bounced her fuzzy brown terrier body which was smaller than Arnold with his long regal black fur. Arnold sat expectantly with his golden eyes glowing with anticipation.

"There's no help for it, guys, I have to use this front room as a kitchen until the construction is done."

Ozzy bounded off with her treat. She was so friendly and content to play by herself with her toys. Which helped me feel better because I was at the diner so much these days.

In humorous contrast, Arnold sat there expectantly.

"Do you want a treat, buddy?" I pulled out two of them and put them on the floor. I knew better than to ask him to do something, like beg for the treat. He'd likely suffocate me in my sleep with his furry body if I did that.

I washed the treat dust off my hands in the small bathroom under the stairs and went back to my onions. The beginnings of a soup I hoped to perfect for the diner. I loved working for Aerie at the Soup and Scoop as a cook, which I was extremely grateful for. I desperately needed the money to fix the kitchen and get back to flipping this house. My plan was to move on to the next big flip so I could finally show my sister that I could be independent. Truly independent without receiving constant input from my big sister.

As if on cue, my cell phone rang. I stopped stirring the onions and closed my eyes. It would not surprise me in the least if it was her.

I reached in my pocket and pulled out the phone. Sure enough, my sister's somber, meditative face stared at me from my cell phone, her name in bold at the top of the screen: Darla Damian. It was her "stage" name. Her nom de plume, her fake front. I sighed. She wasn't a fake, I had to admit. She was a real-deal psychic, and she made her fortune doing it. I just wished she'd leave me out of it. I wanted nothing to do with the family "inheritance." She swore I had the gift too, but I don't. Well, except for hearing my cat's voice in my mind telling me important things like the discount cat food I dared to buy him was stale or the heating mat in his kitty bed needed to be turned on. As if on cue, Arnold chimed in. *Why won't you answer Darla?*

I remembered Arnold told me I sighed audibly whenever Darla called, so he always knew. I ignored the call, letting it roll to voicemail. "I don't need Darla telling me all the reasons I shouldn't have moved here." She had micromanaged me since we were kids. Having a sister who could sense the future and truly knew it was annoying on so many levels.

Immediately the phone rang again. I seriously contemplated blocking her calls, but this time it wasn't her number on the phone screen. It was an unknown number.

"Hello?"

"Is this Mira Michaels?"

"Yes."

"This is Elaine Dunbar, from the cat show. You rescued Oksana for me."

"Oh, hi. How are you and how's Oksana?"

"That's what I'd like to talk to you about. Thank you again for saving Oksana. I don't really know how to tell you this, but we have a situation."

Elaine explained the situation in far more detail than necessary. All the while I marched through the house to hunt down Arnold. Just as I was ending the call, I backtracked and found him lying innocently in a dollop of sunshine, near the porch window.

"You've got some explaining to do."

Hmm? *I'm napping.* His fluffy black fur barely moved.

3

"I just got a call asking me to go 50-50 on vet bills for your little friend Oksana."

His head snapped toward me. *Is she injured?*

"No, you naughty cat, she's going to have kittens! And you're responsible."

Really? That's wonderful news. He relaxed into the sunshine.

"Do you know how many mouths that is to feed?"

Doesn't the mother feed them?

"Ooh, Arnold you are on my last nerve. How could you do this?"

I could have sworn he grinned. *It was easy.*

I shook my head and forced myself to do some deep breathing exercises that Aerie taught in her yoga classes. Breathe in. Breathe out. Not much I could do about kittens. Or paying for future vet bills. I sighed and went back to my soup before I burned another batch of onions.

EARLY MONDAY MORNING at the diner had its own flow, and Aerie and I had just begun when my cell phone rang. My sister, again. I had lost count of how many times she called yesterday. She was nothing if not persistent. I turned off the phone's ringer and stuffed it back into my pocket. She wasn't going to stop calling until I answered. I wasn't in the mood for her brand of lecture.

Aerie looked up from the computer at the cash register, her blond hair pulled back in a snug ponytail. "Who are you ignoring?"

"Ignoring? Oh, it's my sister."

I shrugged it off. I needed to start a new soup recipe and I was really worried about how it would taste.

"Siblings are important. Maybe she needs something."

If anyone knew about how annoying siblings could be, it was Aerie. Her brother, Jay, was dating the girl who bullied Aerie all through middle school. Definite conflict there. "She doesn't need anything. She never needs anything from me. Except to give me a lecture. And I need to focus on our new soup this morning."

Aerie shrugged. "Okay, but you know your sister is with you your whole life. You should find ways to make your relationship work for each other."

I raised an eyebrow. "Are you taking up psychology?"

"Meditation gives me insight." She stretched her arms and smiled. "What soup are you making today?"

"Hungarian mushroom." I took a deep breath. "I made a small batch at home and it tasted really good. But I don't know if I can increase the amount for the diner and have it still be tasty."

"I have faith in you. You can do it."

"Thanks, Mama Duck."

"Mama Duck?" She gave me a confused look.

"You know that little picture book about Quack the duck who's afraid to swim?" I couldn't help but smile at the recollection of my own mother reading it to me and Darla. "She tells him she has faith that he can do it. And he does."

"I will happily be your Mama Duck."

"Thanks." I grabbed an apron off the hook and walked into the refrigerator. This soup would taste great. I hoped. I filled Aerie in on Arnold's antics and the kitten fiasco, while we got ready for the breakfast rush. "I love kittens. Will the owner let you keep one, do you think?"

"That's the least of my worries at this point. I need to figure out how to pay the vet bills until the glorious day." I went back to focusing on my prep work.

I had to admit I was getting better at cooking over-easy eggs and keeping the bacon grease from burning down the diner. I still hadn't mastered pancake pouring but at least I wasn't undercooking them anymore. And now I understood why toast was always served cold in restaurants. You could never time it properly in order to have the toast pop by the time the egg was done on the grill. At least I could stick it under the heat lamp while I finished cooking the egg.

I was getting to like small-town living. I knew almost everyone's name who came in and they now knew me. Of course, the murder in my house had mostly helped with my celebrity.

Mr. Meyer smiled and held up the toast with his melted butter on it. He appreciated the effort.

Aside from a few patrons like Mr. Meyer, the Monday breakfast rush had been mostly to-go coffee-drinkers. It let me get ready for the real rush, everyone came in for lunch.

Aerie finished bussing the dining room while I started to prep the mushroom soup. I propped my phone on the shelf above the stove and read the recipe, careful to make sure my phone was on vibrate. Maybe I should just block Darla's calls altogether, maybe for just a little while.

First step: chop and sauté onions. Easy enough. I planned to quadruple the recipe. I did the math in my head and grabbed four large, sweet onions. I halved and peeled them and began chopping. We had started using sweet onions last week when we realized I didn't cry as much while I chopped them. It made me a little antsy to be bleary-eyed while handling a sharp knife near my fingers. Switching to sweet onions also seemed to make everything taste better.

I turned on the burner and listened to the gas pop as it

lit under the large soup pot on the stove. I drizzled in the extra-virgin olive oil and allowed it to heat up.

My knife skills were not professional. It took me a while to chop the onions, but it was extremely satisfying to hear them sizzle when I dropped them into the hot oil.

I stirred them briefly with the long bamboo spoon. Then I headed to the walk-in refrigerator for the mushrooms. I had four pounds of cremini mushrooms to chop. And a handful of dry mushrooms that would need to soak. The dry mushrooms were easy enough. I just poured hot water from the percolator over them in a dish. They would have to sit and wait until they softened enough for me to chop them. But I looked down at the four large containers of mushrooms. They were covered in soil. Rinsing them wouldn't be quick.

I grabbed the largest colander from one of the bottom shelves and took it to the sink. I could only dump one container of mushrooms at a time into the colander. I turned the sprayer on and realized I had to rub each and every mushroom until it was clean. I definitely did not want grit to ruin my soup.

I let out a huge sigh as I washed the final batch of mushrooms. I now had a huge counter full of clean mushrooms to chop. I glanced up at the clock--already 11:15. Where had the time gone?

"Aerie! I need help with the mushrooms."

I didn't hear anything from the dining room. I dried off my hands and walked out to the counter. The room was completely empty. "Where did she go?" If I wanted to get the soup ready for lunch, I couldn't look for her. I sent her a quick text and then got back to the kitchen.

I needed to chop fast. While keeping all my fingers. After trying to pin the mushrooms down at an angle and slice them quickly, I decided to pull off all the stems and set them aside. That way I could lay the caps flat on the cutting board and chop them in rows. It seemed to be a more efficient way to chop everything, but it still took time. If today was like a normal Monday, customers would start to arrive around 11:30.

As the board filled with chopped mushrooms, I threw them into the pot and stirred with the bamboo spoon.

I had to watch the heat of the pot. I couldn't risk burning the onions. I added some water and continued chopping.

My mind wandered. It wasn't like Aerie to take off and leave me to fend for myself. She knew I wasn't adept yet in the kitchen and often needed another set of hands. Where was she and why hadn't she let me know she was leaving? This was not like her.

2

The bell over the door rang. Across the room Mrs. Orsa stepped into the diner. I abandoned the mushroom soup prep and headed out to the dining room to take her order.

"Good morning, Ms. Michaels, I hope your morning went well."

"You can call me Mira, Mrs.Orsa. What can I get you?" I quickly wiped my mushroom-covered hands on the towel tucked into my apron.

Mrs. Orsa looked me up and down, noticing my frazzled state. "Where is Aerie? Shouldn't she be taking orders?"

I looked around again hoping to see Aerie pop up from under a table or something. No such luck. Mrs. Orsa settled into one of the booths.

"I'm not sure where she went, but that's okay." I hoped. "I can take your order, no problem."

"I'll just have whatever soup you have today and a roll with butter." She straightened her napkin and silverware.

I fidgeted. "Oh, well, I haven't been able to finish it yet. Can I get you something else?"

"Do you have soup leftover from yesterday? That would hit the spot."

"Yes, we have a little left. Tomato bisque. I'll bring that right out for you, Mrs. Orsa."

As I turned toward the kitchen, Mike from the post office came in. "Can I get a turkey club sandwich with extra mayo?"

"Sure, Mike. I'll start that up and be right back with water for both of you." I glanced at Mrs. Orsa who was patiently organizing the contents of her purse.

I went back through the kitchen to the walk-in refrigerator to grab the container of yesterday's tomato bisque. It was just enough for one or two bowls, which should work for Mrs. Orsa. I also took out the turkey and some bacon. The bell on the door rang. "Please let it be Aerie," I mumbled. I peeked out, no such luck. It was two gentlemen I had never seen before. They came in and sat at the counter, chatting as they read through the menu.

After heating Mrs. Orsa's soup and finishing assembling Mike's turkey club, I headed out with both trays and realized I needed to grab them each a water.

I placed the meals on the table. "Water is coming right up," I said to Mrs. Orsa. I smiled at the two men at the counter. Grabbing four water glasses from the stacking crates, I filled them at the fountain. I needed to get back to the soup. One of the glasses fumbled and it landed on the floor with a crash. All conversation stopped.

"No worries everyone, I'm fine." Just then Aerie appeared at the doorway, her golden hair falling out of her hair tie with leaves stuck in it. There was even a scratch on her cheek. She ran over to me and took up one of the rags to clean the floor. We gingerly picked up pieces of glass. "I am so sorry, Mira. Jay texted that he was at your place and accidentally let out Ozzy. I helped him find her."

I sat back on my heels. "Is she okay?"

Aerie let out a big sigh. "Yes. She's back in the house. I gave Jay a good talking to about being careless enough to let the dog out."

Jay had been helping to fix my kitchen ever since the fire. But recently he made it a point to work on it when I wasn't at home. Backlash from accusing him of murder, I guess. I'd have to live with it.

The bell on the diner door rang again and in stepped Chelsea. She was the former middle school bully dating Jay, and the other reason Jay was less than social with both me and Aerie. We didn't exactly approve, and neither of us were subtle about it.

"Do you want me to take her order?" I asked Aerie. I knew her feelings towards Chelsea were still bitter even after all this time. I guess that was the downfall to small town life, running into your past, and a former bully, in your own diner.

"No, I'm an adult. I can handle this. And I promise I won't spit in her water." She smiled darkly.

I gave her a hard look. "You better not." Aerie was normally a very sweet and kind person. Chelsea brought out a different side of her.

Maybe I would bring Chelsea her water.

I took the remaining three glasses of water and made sure that Mrs. Orsa, Mike, and at least one of the guys at the counter had something to drink.

"I can get the rest. Go back into the kitchen." Aerie waved me away with the damp towel. Something was burning in the kitchen. The scent of it wafted into the dining room.

"Thanks." I made a beeline for the pot, I stirred, and realized onions and mushrooms were sticking to the bottom. I added more water and prayed nothing had burned. Hopefully it was just a bit more caramelized. I finished chopping the mushrooms and tossed them into the pot. I finished adding the rest of the ingredients and realized I had to make the béchamel sauce; a thick milk soup made with flour and butter: the cream part of the Hungarian cream of mushroom soup. I grabbed a smaller pot. Smaller being relative; it was still bigger than Arnold's attitude, and placed it on the burner next to the giant soup pot. I melted the butter and walked over to the bench to measure the flour.

Aerie called in from the dining room. "Mira, what's the soup of the day?"

"Hungarian cream of mushroom. But it's not quite ready."

If I would ever get it ready. I closed my eyes and said a quick prayer. "I think I can have it ready in about ten minutes."

I thought that was pushing it but if I hurried, I might be able to do it. I almost scorched the butter; I needed to watch the heat.

After almost burning the béchamel sauce twice more, I added the final ingredient: paprika. A few minutes of cooking time and then we could serve it.

I peered through the window past the counter where the two men sat and talked, then glanced at the clock that hung on the front wall of the dining room. The lunch hour was almost over.

Aerie popped in and asked, "Mr. Walburn is waiting on the soup."

"Oh, okay." I quickly dished out a large bowl and put it on a platter.

"I didn't want to make you nervous."

"Why would I be nervous?"

"Mr. Walburn is the town paper's food critic."

"And Chelsea wants a bowl too." Aerie glanced over her shoulder. "If you ask me, I think she's being way too flirty with Mr. Walburn."

"Oh." I glanced at the soup as Aerie walked it out of the kitchen. I hadn't even tasted it.

I grabbed a spoon and dipped it into the pot and took a quick taste. It needed more salt. But it was passable. And I realized Aerie swept out of the kitchen without getting Chelsea a bowl. I filled another bowl and brought it out to the counter. Chelsea sat a little too close to Mr. Walburn and giggled at something he said. His friend seemed interested too but just grinned and sipped his water.

As Mr. Walburn lifted the spoon to his mouth, I realized I forgot the dried mushrooms. I raced back into the kitchen and grabbed the bowl. Before he or Chelsea could say anything, I scooped out a few mushrooms and added it to their bowls. They lay on the thick soup beautifully and Mr. Walburn smiled. Brought the spoon to his mouth and paused. "It smells heavenly. I'm glad I waited."

I couldn't help but beam with pride at the compliment. I felt my cheeks blush and quickly went back into the kitchen to hide.

The diner slowly emptied. For all of my effort no one else ordered the soup. We could keep it on the menu for tomorrow, but I guessed I had my own suppers squared away for the next few days at least.

I supposed I should thank Mr. Walburn for his kind

words on my soup. A good review would really help Aerie's business.

I finished cleaning and organizing the kitchen, also known as stalling. When it was as clean as I could make it, I walked past Aerie who was hauling in a bucket full of dishes. I wanted to thank Mr. Walburn all the while I was nervously wringing a dish towel.

He and his friend were talking amicably. Chelsea was still there but she had barely touched the soup. She looked at me as though I had tried to feed her pig slop. I returned the look. I wiped down the counter, throwing out her balled-up napkin. Gross. She opened a mirror and fixed her lipstick. Ignoring her, I focused on Mr. Walburn, "I hope you enjoyed your soup."

"I certainly did. The subtle taste of paprika... and I believe you added some smoked paprika as well, was a wonderful touch." He cleared his throat.

"Could I have a glass of water please?"

"I'll try not to drop it this time." I smiled at him. He and his friend chuckled.

I refilled his glass and set it on the counter. He looked a little overheated even though the temperature in the diner was cool. He sipped the glass of water, coughed once, and fell off his stool, hitting the floor with a thud.

After a lot of chaos and a fair amount of screaming from Chelsea, the paramedics arrived. They announced what was pretty clear to me. I had just witnessed my second dead body in two weeks. Chelsea looked down in shock at her bowl of soup, stared me straight in the face, and said to the paramedics. "I think it was the soup. I don't feel very well." She swooned. I wondered if she had practiced that. The paramedics asked us all to leave what now seemed to be a crime scene and helped Chelsea out to the back of the ambulance. They hovered around her, taking her blood pressure and vitals.

Dan Lockheart showed up. As the town's only detective and acting chief of police, Dan appeared whenever there was a question of crime. I'd heard others say he was nice to look at, and yeah, maybe his eyes were dreamy, but all I noticed was how annoying he was when I was trying to get things done. After quickly speaking with the paramedics, he made a beeline for me. "I heard there was some question about the soup?"

"That's just Chelsea being melodramatic." I leaned on the outside wall of the diner. My feet ached.

"They're taking her to the hospital to have her stomach pumped."

"I hope she enjoys the ramifications of that decision," Aerie said. "I just wish I could be there." She folded her arms across her chest, and I elbowed her. She realized she was talking to a detective and not just her friend Dan and closed her mouth.

But it wasn't as if Detective Lockheart hadn't noticed. He raised an eyebrow at Aerie's obvious dislike of the woman.

"Not a fan of Ms. Smith dating your brother?"

I jumped in. "Are we sure Mr. Walburn didn't die of natural causes? Aerie wouldn't have done anything to make Chelsea sick." Well, I didn't think she would.

"I certainly hope not." Detective Lockheart gave her a quick glance. Aerie blushed, turned away, and sat down on the bench outside the diner. "And, yes, *we*, meaning paramedics and actual police officers trained to solve crimes, have found evidence with the body that there may have been foul play." He waved to some arriving officers to go into the diner.

"Just once I'd like to show up to a crime scene and not find you standing over a murder victim, Ms. Michaels." He pinched his nose and sighed. "But I'll settle for a statement from each of you about what happened here today." He pulled out a notepad. He gave directions to the crime scene photographer. Then he started the statement-taking.

"Mr. Walburn had the mushroom soup?"

I nodded. "Yes, I made it today, so it's fresh."

"I'll need to bag it up as evidence. We will need to have it tested." He nodded to another officer.

"I put every ingredient in there. I know there's nothing in it that would poison him."

"Ms. Michaels. My job is to look at every possibility."

"But shouldn't you be looking at his enemies or something?"

"He's a food critic. If he had an enemy, it could be you, a chef at a local restaurant."

I rolled my eyes. "I didn't even know he was a food critic."

"So you say."

"Detective Lockheart. You're making it very difficult for me to stay civil with you."

"My job isn't to be your friend or play nice. My job is to investigate this crime to the best of my ability. And catch the bad guys." He gave me a penetrating look that lasted a little too long.

I held his gaze. "You're still mad that I solved Robbie's kidnapping and Becca's murder."

"I am not." He shifted on his feet.

"Yes, you are. I can see it. You're mad that I, a woman with no detective experience, did your job better than you could."

"Right now, Ms. Michaels, you are the prime suspect in a murder investigation. I highly recommend that you cooperate and otherwise keep your mouth shut."

Rage built up inside me like a pressure cooker. "Keep my mouth shut?" I pushed off from the wall and stepped toward the detective when Aerie snagged my arm and pulled me away.

The detective walked past us and into the diner. He turned and held the door. "Don't leave until I get your statements." He let the door close behind him.

I glared at his back through the glass.

Aerie put her hands on my shoulders. "Dan is right. We're suspects in a murder. And it's best if we don't anger the one man that can prove that we are not."

I breathed in. I breathed out. Gaining my composure, I nodded. "You're right." I collected myself, straightened my shirt, tightened the apron strings, and walked in to face the detective.

I could give him a statement through gritted teeth if I had to.

And I had to.

Detective Lockheart crouched near the body taking notes. I cleared my throat and he stood but continued to look down at the body. "I can give you my statement now," I said. Aerie took a seat behind me in a show of solidarity.

He flipped to a new page in his notebook. "I need to know every single step of your preparation of the meal that this man ate. Was there anything that struck you as odd about his behavior or anyone else's?"

I thought for a moment. "I can't say that anything was odd. Aerie can tell you more about their interactions. I can tell you about when they came in, and that he ordered the mushroom soup. I was behind schedule with the soup so only he and Chelsea were the ones to order it and eat it."

"Chelsea's vitals are concerning, so the paramedics are taking her to the hospital."

He was treating Chelsea's illness seriously. Maybe my estimation that she was faking it to get attention was wrong. I glanced over at Aerie to see her reaction. She just rolled her eyes.

"I'll be following up with her as soon as I'm done here."

"She barely touched the soup." I informed the detective.

"Which might be why she's still alive."

"Look Detective Lockheart, I don't appreciate you insinuating that I have poisoned people with my soup."

"It's looking like that might be what has happened here."

"Well, it didn't. And I can prove it to you."

"You will do no such thing. You will leave the detective work to me."

"I need to clear my name."

"I can arrest you for impeding an investigation."

"You wouldn't dare."

Detective Lockheart's left eyebrow raised. "Oh, wouldn't I?"

"Don't threaten me. I know my rights. I haven't done anything wrong."

"I can have you brought to the station. And if you don't cooperate, I can put you in jail."

Aerie stood up from her chair. "Mira."

I took a deep breath, and I closed my eyes, mostly so I could stop looking at Detective Dan's face. I turned around and marched myself out of the front door of the diner.

It had begun to rain and I could feel the little patters of water as they hit the top of my head. I imagined the water sizzling and steaming as if on a hot pan. Because that certainly felt like what my brain was doing right now. I was so angry that Detective Lockheart would threaten me with jail. I probably could solve this case without him. I did it last time. I heard the door to the diner open behind me. I turned. It was Aerie. "I think you and Dan should steer clear of each other as much as humanly possible."

"You think?" I swiped at a raindrop on my cheek.

"Mira. He is the only person that can prove we're innocent. I'm just as much a suspect as you are. And if I lose this business..." She took a deep breath. "I won't be able to keep the house."

Reality hit hard. I wouldn't be able to keep my house either if I lost my job at the Soup and Scoop.

"I'm sorry, Aerie." I turned and looked at the diner. "I'll try to rein in my anger when I'm around Detective Lockheart. Although maybe it's best if you supervise."

She smiled. "He pushes your buttons."

I didn't understand her tone. "Oh, you think so?"

"I think he's just doing his job."

I let out a long sigh. I looked up at the cloudy sky and let the rain fall on my face. I took another deep breath and met Aerie's gaze. "I will stay out of Detective Lockheart's way. I promise. I won't let anything happen to the Soup and Scoop." I took her hand and gave it a reassuring squeeze.

She nodded and closed her eyes. "But maybe..."

"Maybe we should go visit Chelsea in the hospital? Because maybe she's responsible for all this?"

"I wouldn't put it past her."

"But we're not investigating in any way," I said.

"She *is* my brother's girlfriend." Aerie said, innocently.

"That's right. And we're just checking on her to make sure she's okay," I recited.

"Is there anything inside the diner that you need?" Aerie asked.

"No. I have my cell phone, that's it." I pulled it out of my back pocket to show her. "Never leave home without it." I kept a credit card and my driver's license in my cell phone's case.

"I'll get my car keys and my purse."

We rode to the hospital in relative silence. Both of us knew what was on the line. Aerie turned into the drive that led to the hospital. "I wouldn't put it past Chelsea to do something like this."

"She's that mean and vindictive?"

"Yes. I know from personal experience."

"She was a bully as a kid. Is she really that nasty now?" I looked at her. "I mean nasty enough to ruin your life?"

"You and I have both been very openly antagonistic toward her relationship with my brother."

"That's true. But think about it, would she do something that would hurt her boyfriend's sister? Wouldn't it possibly have some backlash if her boyfriend got angry about it?"

"I bet Chelsea believes she could sweet-talk her way out of anything."

Aerie parked the car in the visitor's lot. "I guess we're about to find out."

"I don't care how sick she is, she's telling us what happened."

We walked into the hospital with a mission. To find out what happened. And we bumped into a man and woman on their way out. The woman was sobbing on the man's shoulder as he held her up.

"I'm so sorry. We should really watch where we're going." I shot Aerie a glance.

The woman composed herself quickly and appeared to recognize Aerie. "You run the diner." She pointed at me. "And you're the cook, aren't you? You're the one who poisoned my husband."

"I did no such thing. That soup is perfectly fine."

"You poisoned him." She gripped the man's arm fiercely. "Terry, take me out of here before I do something."

The man nodded and walked Mrs. Walburn out of the hospital. I watched as the automatic doors swooshed closed and they disappeared into the parking lot.

"Well. That happened." I shook off the huge bolt of negative energy that seemed to have hit me like a brick. "I've never been directly accused of murder before."

"She was very melodramatic. I guess today she has a reason to be." We made our way up to the second floor where the nurse at the receiving desk said we could find Chelsea. When we walked in she was on her phone swiping left. She looked alert and oriented to me. At least until she saw us, then suddenly her demeanor became quite the opposite. She swooned and laid back into her pillow moaning.

Aerie was the first in the room. "Give it up. We saw you."

Chelsea sat up straighter. "Your cook fed me slop. They had to pump my stomach. Do you know how humiliating that is?"

"If you hadn't gone all melodramatic on the paramedics you wouldn't have had to have your stomach pumped."

"Because the soup was not poisoned," I added.

"I know you both hate me," she whined.

"We don't hate you," I said. Aerie made a dismissive noise.

Chelsea raised an eyebrow. "You want me out of your brother's life. It's not going to happen."

"I do want you out of my brother's life. But I'm not going to hurt you to do it."

"Oh, wouldn't you?" Chelsea sat up and glared.

"You're insane."

I stepped between the two women before it became an all-out brawl. "Look Chelsea, we came down first to see if you're okay." Aerie made another noise. "And then we wanted to ask you what you remember about sitting with Mr. Walburn. Was there anything suspicious going on?"

"No. Not a thing." Chelsea adroitly turned her head, looked up at the ceiling and pinched her lips as if she had no more to say.

"That's a flat-out lie. I saw you flirting obnoxiously with him."

Chelsea turned back and glared at Aerie. "I was not. And don't you dare say anything to Jay about it.

"And what if I do?"

"You don't think I have him wrapped around my finger?"

The remark took Aerie aback. She closed her mouth. I stepped forward again. "Look Chelsea, we just want to try to figure out what happened at the diner today. If we don't we could lose the diner and Aerie and Jay could lose their house."

"Jay doesn't want that house anyway. We're buying our own house together."

I could almost swear I heard retching noises from Aerie. Obviously, coming to the hospital was a bad idea.

"Fine. If you can't help us, we'll leave."

"Good. Sayonara, sister." She snapped her hand like an alligator mouth in my direction. I couldn't help but dislike Chelsea just a little bit more. I took Aerie by the arm and we walked out the door.

"Well, that was worthless."

"I wouldn't say that. Chelsea did tell us Jay doesn't want to own the house anymore. That makes me think she is still the suspect because if you and Jay can't own the house anymore that makes him free to purchase said home with her."

"I. Hate. Her," Aerie enunciated slowly.

"All right. Let's get out of here. I think we need to find out how Mr. Walburn was poisoned. That will help us figure out what Chelsea did. Do you think she actually took some of the poison herself?"

"Only one way to find out."

Aerie went to the nurse's station and as sweetly as I've

ever seen her, asked on behalf of her dear friend Chelsea, if they found any poison in her system. She just wanted to make sure that her dear friend Chelsea, was going to be okay. I had to give it to Aerie. She had some excellent acting skills.

Aerie walked swiftly down the hallway. "Come on, let's go."

"What did you find out?" Aerie just shook her head. We walked all the way back to the car in silence.

Once we were seated and buckled, I turned to her. "Okay, spill it. What did you find out?"

"She had traces of poison in her system." I sucked in a breath. Aerie continued. "But only traces."

I sat back in the seat. Shocked. My mushroom soup was poisoned? "How?"

"That's what we need to find out."

4

The next morning, Aerie called to say that Dan was still investigating, and the diner had to remain closed, so I made a much-needed run to the grocery store. I came home from the supermarket and heard pounding in the vicinity of my still-under-construction kitchen. After the fire last month, Jay had sworn he would help fix it. Which I was really grateful for, because I didn't have the money yet to pay him. He even agreed to this after I had unceremoniously accused him of the murder of Rebecca Branson, the woman found dead in my kitchen.

Jay and I had actually gotten along pretty well when he first started working here. But that changed after he announced he was dating Chelsea. I was surprised that he hadn't mentioned it earlier to me, but then, we had just met. It was my own fault for crushing on him so soon after moving here. I had to agree with Aerie though, Chelsea was not my favorite person.

It was nice to know he stuck to his promises and continued to work on the kitchen despite everything. Such a good guy.

I put all the groceries down on the makeshift dining room table, a card table I had found in the basement, and emptied the bags, adding things to the mini-fridge.

More hammering pounded on the other side of the wall. It sounded like he was working on the structure for the walls.

The pounding stopped. It was replaced by a knock on the ply board nailed between the dining room and the unfinished kitchen. He cleared his throat on the other side. "Do you mind if I come in?"

"Sure, I'll meet you at the front door." I shoved the rest of the groceries in the mini-fridge and stood up to get the door.

I held the storm door open as Jay walked in. He stood with his feet together right in front of the doorway, unmoving. His close-clipped beard and rugged good looks still made me a bit weak in the knees. He stared straight ahead. "I don't think I'll be able to finish the kitchen."

"What?" I was totally confused.

"I can't keep working here. I can find somebody who will."

"Jay, what's going on?"

He looked at me, surprised. "You think I could keep working here after what happened yesterday?"

"What do you mean?"

"Chelsea is in the hospital, because someone tried to poison her."

"And you think that person is me?"

"I don't know who it is. If it was you, or if Aerie put you up to it..." He shook his head.

"Jay, we had nothing to do with poisoning Chelsea or Mr. Walburn." I stared right back at him. "And I'm more than a little upset that you would think so."

"You're the one who made the soup," he countered.

I closed my eyes and took a breath. It did appear that the mushroom soup was poisoned. And until we had the lab results back, I wouldn't know for sure. But I did know that I didn't poison that soup. For the smallest second, I wondered if Aerie was responsible. She was the only person in the kitchen other than me. I tried to crush the idea. I couldn't even imagine it. But somehow it stayed. Maybe because Jay thought it could happen, that it was a possibility.

"I swear to you Jay, I didn't poison the soup."

He looked into my eyes for a long moment. "Regardless, I can't keep working on the kitchen. I'll find somebody to do it for you."

I nodded.

On his way out the door, he said something over his shoulder: "If I do find out you or Aerie had anything to do with this..." He shook his head, didn't finish the thought, but simply walked to his truck.

The engine revved as he drove off. I closed the door and leaned on it, taking a deep breath.

Well, touché. I figured he owed me that one. After I blamed him for murder last month, he blamed me for murder this month. We had an interesting relationship. But I doubted I would see him again for a long while. It made me sad. I looked down to find Arnold gently rubbing against my shins. *He likes you.*

"I wouldn't be so sure about that."

He likes you.

Arnold didn't expound on that fact, maybe he just "knew" but I refused to even toy with the idea that my cat could be psychic. Arnold rubbed against my leg again.

"Do you want some snacks, buddy? I could use one myself."

I rummaged through the remaining grocery bags and

found the crinkly plastic bag of treats. The sound that would get him to run to me from anywhere in the house. I gave him a handful. I needed comfort food, too. I searched through the grocery bags for something for myself to munch on and settled on a bag of chips. As I popped a potato chip in my mouth, I realized I needed to sit down with Aerie and figure out who was in the diner that afternoon and who would want to see Mr. Walburn dead. Chelsea had her own history. But if somebody had wanted her out of the picture, most likely she would be in the same situation as Mr. Walburn. Unless the killer had missed the mark.

We needed to start a list. Aerie would have all of the receipts from those who had lunch at the diner yesterday.

I grabbed my cell phone to call her and it buzzed in my hand. I dropped the phone and it thankfully bounced lightly on the new area rug I had recently added to the room courtesy of Aerie's basement. I leaned down and picked up the phone.

It was a text.

From my sister. Impeccable timing as usual.

I read it before I could ignore it. Now I was angry with the notification screen on my phone. I made a mental note to change the settings on my text app.

She always knew how to get a reaction.

It read, *Are you in trouble?*

Nope. Not at all. Just the prime suspect in a murder investigation. Thanks for reminding me.

AERIE ARRIVED QUICKLY--MORE QUICKLY than I would have expected for her to load the receipts into a spreadsheet. She explained that Dan had asked for the list as a part of the investigation and she kept a copy. She handed me the spreadsheet and put a tray of vegan chocolate chip cookies on the table.

"Jay is pretty mad about the two of us visiting Chelsea yesterday."

"Yeah."

"He came home and packed an overnight bag and moved out. Again. He's always doing this. I know he thinks he needs space, but I hate it. I think he's staying with Chelsea, now that she's out of the hospital."

"He moved out? Oh, Air, I'm so sorry." I put down the pack of pens that I had been holding. "He was over here this morning. He actually thinks we had something to do with Chelsea getting sick."

"That would mean he thinks we killed Mr. Walburn. Jay is just being crazy. That's the Chelsea effect." She waved it off.

But I still couldn't shake it. The best thing we could do right now was to look at the group of possible suspects that had lunch at the diner yesterday. The only thing I knew for certain was that I didn't put any poison in the soup.

"So how many people are we looking at?"

Aerie scanned the document. "Well, including you and me, there were eight people in the diner when Mr. Walburn...fell off his stool."

I took out a notebook, opened to an empty page, and grabbed one of the pens.

"Mr. Walburn had the soup and a glass of water. Mr. Belinsky, his friend, had a hamburger and fries, and there was Chelsea who, surprisingly, also had the mushroom soup. Ellie Bracken came in to grab a sandwich and left." I wrote down the names. I also crossed off Mrs. Orsa. I figured there was a limit of one murder per family. But then I thought better of it. Thinking like a detective meant everyone there was a suspect and we needed to clear each name no matter who they were. I glanced over at Aerie, planning to tell her this, but she seemed to be puzzling something out. "What is it?"

"There was also a Mr. Andrews, Sam Andrews." She grabbed her phone and searched for something.

"What's up?"

"I actually think Sam Andrews owns the Pizza Pub in the next town over." She tapped her screen. "Yep. Here he is. The owner of the Pizza Pub."

"What's he doing at your restaurant if he owns one of his own?"

"That's a good question."

"I think we might have found suspect number one."

"Do you think Mr. Walburn gave the Pizza Pub a bad review?"

"It's a definite possibility. We'll need to pull the past newspaper articles and see what we find."

I went up to my bedroom to grab my laptop so we could do the search more easily than on our phones. When I came back down the stairs, I heard voices in the dining room. I came around the corner and found Aerie talking to a young man wearing work boots. They looked up when I arrived. Aerie introduced us.

"This is Devon. He works with Jay."

I nodded. That was quick. Now I knew I wouldn't be seeing Jay anytime soon.

We needed to figure out who poisoned Chelsea and Mr. Walburn so Jay could stop suspecting not only me, but his sister, too.

I shook Devon's hand. "Thanks for coming by, Devon. I really appreciate it."

"Not a problem. Lead the way to the kitchen." Devon was heavily muscled and probably not too many years past high school. He wore the same kind of work boots as Jay. I wondered if I'd always take note of people's choice in boots.

"Normally through there," I said, "but it's boarded up for now. There's access through the backyard."

He nodded. "Okay. I'll head outside."

"Just let me know if you need anything."

"Will do."

Devon disappeared around the corner of the house and I closed the front door.

Aerie and I sat on the floor in the dining room looking over the list of suspects while I booted my computer.

Aerie grabbed the notebook. "We should rank the suspects on who we think could have done it."

I nodded. "I'll put Mr. Belinsky as number two. They always say it's someone you know." I grinned sardonically. We had all known the murderer last month and if they could be a killer, anyone could be.

"In that case, don't forget about his wife." The voice came from the other side of the plywood. Both Aerie and I started. Neither of us realized that Devon could hear us.

But then I thought about it and shouted back. "Why would his wife kill him?"

"Oh, well maybe not the wife. But I know a lot of guys in town who wished she was single."

"Like who?" I shouted.

Devon rattled off a long list of names. "

"Okay, okay. We get it. Thanks, Devon."

I switched gears and pulled up the archived food critic

files of the Paradise Pond Independent. It took a bit of scrolling, but I finally found his review of the Pizza Pub.

"Found it."

"What does it say?"

I made a face. "Not good. 'I've tasted better pizza made out of cardboard.' Yikes."

Aerie nibbled a cookie. "I'm kind of glad he didn't have time to publish a review of the Soup and Scoop."

"Don't let Dan hear you say that."

"Yeah, yeah. It doesn't really matter; the damage is done."

"What do you mean?"

"No one is going to want to eat at the Soup and Scoop, maybe ever again." Aerie finished off the cookie and frowned.

"How long do you think it will take to get the tests back on the mushroom soup?" I grabbed a cookie and nibbled.

"You actually think that will clear us?"

"Won't it?"

"Of the murder, but not necessarily in the opinion of the rest of the town. Someone dropped dead while eating our food."

"You don't think people will come back to the diner?"

Aerie shook her head. "I don't know. But I am worried. And I still wouldn't put it past Chelsea to have orchestrated this whole thing to put me out of business so she could get at Jay."

"Well, the sooner we solve this, the sooner it's behind us." I didn't like seeing Aerie this upset.

"You saw her flirting with Mr. Walburn, didn't you?"

"I did. But that doesn't make her a killer."

"Well, maybe she screwed it up and accidentally killed Mr. Walburn instead of just making him sick."

"Okay," I conceded, "but I still think we should keep Sam Andrews in mind. It is very odd that he would be at the Soup and Scoop on the same day as the murder."

"Okay, fine, keep him on the list. But I'd love to see Chelsea behind bars."

The look in Aerie's eyes worried me.

AFTER AERIE LEFT, I spent a long time pondering the thought that bothered me. She had been a little too aggressive in her dislike of Chelsea and too eager to see her behind bars. I had to keep the possibility open that Aerie could have something to do with poisoning Chelsea. Although it was really challenging to consider her as a person who would murder someone, even inadvertently. I highly doubted it. Still, I couldn't go to sleep until I made sure.

Once it was dark, I headed to the diner. I wanted to walk through everything that happened yesterday. Step-by-step. My memories were such a blur that I felt I needed to be in the diner to clarify my thoughts.

I put on my favorite black hoodie and a pair of black yoga pants, jammed my cell phone in the side pocket, and made my way to the Soup and Scoop.

The sidewalks and road were still damp, but the rain had finally stopped. Everything had that cool green smell after a hard rain. I took a deep breath and hustled across the street. Aerie had given me a key so that, just like Robbie, the former cook used to, I could open the restaurant while she was teaching her yoga classes each morning.

I ducked around the crime scene tape, let myself in, and quickly closed the door behind me. I stood for a moment in the doorway. The diner looked different in the dark. It smelled faintly of hamburgers and french fries, which made me feel nostalgic.

But I had work to do. I made my way into the kitchen, figuring I would start there and re-imagine the day from the moment when I started the mushroom soup.

I distinctly remembered when Mr. Walburn came in with his friend because I had never seen either of them in the diner before. I walked over to the counter. I remembered dropping the glass and Aerie arriving to help me clean it up. Would that have given someone enough time to poison my soup? I didn't remember anyone pushing past us. I also couldn't remember when Sam Andrews arrived. Aerie must have seated him and taken his order.

Just then a gust of wind came in through the open door and a tall, dark figure stood in the pool of light from the streetlamp. I couldn't see his face, but as soon as he cleared his throat, I knew who it was.

I closed my eyes and took a breath. "Hello, Detective." I waited for his tirade. I didn't have to wait long.

"What are you doing here? This is still an active crime scene."

"I needed to jog my memory on what happened yesterday."

"Or you're here getting rid of evidence. Very suspicious. Also, I told you I would arrest you if I saw you meddling in this investigation."

"I'm not doing anything wrong. In fact, I'm trying to figure out what happened so that my friend can continue to run her business and keep the house she lives in."

"You're one of the key suspects. You being here makes you look even worse."

"Oh, give me a break. You know I didn't do this. What

would be my motive? So I could ruin the diner's reputation?"

"I don't know what the motive is yet. I'm working on it."

"You're working on it? Well, you're taking too long. The longer the diner stays closed the less likely people will come back and eat here."

"They won't come back because you poisoned them."

"Oh, so I'm guilty until proven innocent?"

He shook his head. "I shouldn't have said it that way, I mean someone has poisoned them. What people will think is what people will think."

"Did lab tests show poison in the soup?" My heart raced. If the soup was poisoned and I didn't do it, didn't that mean it must have been Aerie?

"I'm still waiting on the tests." He took a step closer to the counter. "Look, you need to get out of here or I will have to arrest you."

I felt like this was déjà vu. It was as if he and I were reciting lines in a play. Only last time I had been cleaning the counter. Then I remembered that moment, and the crushed-up napkin near Chelsea's plate.

I searched for the trashcan and couldn't find it. "Do you have the trash from yesterday?"

"What are you talking about?"

"In evidence, do you have yesterday's trash?"

"You are not part of this investigation."

"Maybe I should be," I put a hand on my hip, "because you certainly seem to need me."

"You are not needed." His voice became louder. "Now vacate the premises, or I swear, Ms. Michaels, I will arrest you."

"Don't threaten me." I walked around the counter avoiding him. "I'm leaving."

Once I was outside, I tried to shake off all the anger. That man drove me insane. So he still thought I was a suspect? Wait a minute. How did he know I was in the diner tonight? Was he staking out the place? Or me? Both thoughts were unnerving. If he was focused on me as a suspect, he was wasting his time, and I really did need to step up and figure out who actually poisoned people in the Soup and Scoop.

Otherwise, we'd be out of business, or worse yet, in jail.

5

The next morning I woke to the sound of Ozzy yipping to go out. The tiny whine at the end meant it was urgent. I yawned and dragged myself out of bed.

"Come on, little doggie, let's go do business." I could be back in bed in under five minutes if she was quick. A proper walk could happen when the sun had risen above the horizon. Another huge yawn hit me while I zipped up my hoodie.

Ozzy knew what was coming. She jumped and bounced on her tiny feet. "Come on. Let's go." I waved her down the stairs. She yipped, then sped down the stairs and hallway like greased lightning. I yawned again. I couldn't imagine having that much energy. I clipped the leash to her collar, and we headed outside.

Ozzy was a good girl, we didn't have to stroll too far along the front of the house before she paused and peed. I was still half asleep and in the middle of another yawn when I noticed movement over by the Soup and Scoop.

At first, by the color of the woman's hair, I thought it was Aerie. But this woman was shorter. And super suspicious looking, pausing to throw furtive glances over her shoulder every few seconds. Chelsea! Out of the hospital and well enough to lighten her hair color. Oh, joy.

But what was she doing? Taping pieces of paper to the diner? Oh, brother. "Come on Ozzy. Let's go see what she's up to."

Ozzy was more than happy to take a longer walk. I wasn't. Half-asleep and still in my pajama pants, I was in no mood to confront Chelsea. But it would be a cold day in hades when I would let her do anything to the diner. She was wallpapering the glass storefront with black skull and crossbones on noxiously neon green sheets of paper. I rushed over and yelled, "Chelsea. What are you doing?"

She jumped like I had electrocuted her. She clearly didn't count on someone being out this early in the morning. Her eyes landed on me, and she grimaced. "I'm letting other people know what happens when you visit the Soup and Scoop diner. They get poisoned."

"They do not." For the first time, I wished Ozzy was more menacing. Then I could sic her on Chelsea.

"Oh really? Then why did I need to get my stomach pumped?" She slammed another paper to the front window. "And why did Mr. Walburn die?" She dragged out that last word like a soap opera line.

I closed the distance and pulled papers off the building. Ozzy was more than happy to bounce along. She wanted to meet Chelsea and make a new friend.

"Aerie wouldn't put it past you to do this to yourself just to make sure the Soup and Scoop go out of business." I grabbed paper after paper and crunched them up. The papers made a very satisfying sound as I balled them up in my fists.

"Oh, yeah, right, like I would poison myself." She

slammed another page to the wall taking the place of two I had just removed. I grabbed it and tore it down. We squared off shoulders and stared at each other.

A sudden grin flickered across her lips. "You want to go, little girl?"

"Are you kidding me? What are you, gangsta?"

She leaned into my face. "You couldn't take me."

"I could take you out faster than you could blink."

"Alright, ladies. Break it up. It's too early for me to start hauling people to the station. Too much paperwork." Detective Lockheart appeared behind me. I glanced over my shoulder and took a step back when Chelsea actually took a swing at me. She clipped me across my right cheek, barely missing my nose.

"You... I can't believe you swung at me!" But before I could tear her newly golden locks off her head, Detective Lockheart stepped between us and put a hand on my shoulder and the other on Chelsea's. My cheek began to pulse with each pounding heartbeat.

Detective Lockheart cleared his throat. He had a firm grip on both our shoulders. "Ms. Michaels, do you wish to press charges of assault on Ms. Smith?" That sentence took the fire right out of Chelsea. Her stance relaxed immediately. And then her eyes welled up with tears.

I rolled my eyes. "I cannot believe you," I said.

The waterworks had started. She sniffled. "These past couple of days have been so hard on me."

"That's understandable, Ms. Smith. But you've assaulted Ms. Michaels." He turned to me. "Again, do you want to press charges?"

"I'll think about it." I blurted it out in her direction. "Maybe she can remove these signs?" I pointed to the skull and crossbones that littered the front of the building.

39

"Ms. Smith, I expect this to be cleaned up."

She nodded and tears dripped down her cheeks. Detective Lockheart released both our shoulders, now that the threat of a catfight was over.

"Yes, sir." She nodded and sniffled. And she began to peel the signs off the building and retrieve the fallen pages from the sidewalk.

I shook my head. "Unbelievable." I turned to take Ozzy back home.

"Hold on, Ms. Michaels." Detective Lockheart took a few steps in my direction. "I would like to see you down at the station."

"I'm not pressing charges." I didn't need all the hassle. And I was standing in my PJs in the middle of Main Street.

"It's about the investigation." He eyed me coolly up and down. "Meet me at the station as soon as you're...dressed."

"Thanks for your assessment of my attire, Detective Lockheart. I can meet you at the station in an hour." I turned sharply on my heel, tugging patiently at Ozzy's leash because she wanted to make a new friend with Detective Lockheart, and made my way back to the house cursing the entire way.

An hour later I sat across the desk from Detective Lockheart.

"What is this about?"

"I'll be brief. Some new evidence has been found."

"Okay? What is it?"

"It appears that Mr. Walburn had indeed started a review of your cooking at the Soup and Scoop."

"But Monday was his first visit to the restaurant, at least while I was chef."

"Well, obviously he had been there before and was planning to publish a review." He slid a piece of paper across the desk to me. "Here's the beginning of his review."

I scanned the paper. The review was scathing. Enough to put the diner in jeopardy. I shook my head. "I know I've never served him food at the diner before Monday. So, he can't possibly have written this about my cooking."

"The document was date-stamped and was created last week. Prior to his death."

"Again, he hadn't been to the diner. Not since I've been there."

"Okay." Detective Lockheart took a deep breath, clearly trying to explain something I didn't understand. "Let's assume, for argument's sake, that Monday was his first day at the diner. And let's make another assumption and say that he was planning to write this review before even tasting your food."

I didn't care about being calm. "Which is absurd."

"Let me continue. Let's assume, that for whatever reason, Mr. Walburn had decided to write up this bad review prior to even tasting your food. Now, while that makes his character look less than sincere, it does give us motive as to why you would want him dead."

"What?" I leapt to my feet. "What are you talking about? I didn't want the man dead. I didn't even know about this review."

"Maybe he gave you the heads-up about the review. Maybe you simply meant to make him sick. And the prank backfired."

"I don't play pranks."

"But from what I've seen this morning you are capable of retaliatory anger."

"What are you talking about?"

"I believe right before I stepped in at the diner earlier this morning that you would have struck Ms. Smith."

"In self-defense." The words fell out of my mouth before I even realized I had said them.

"And in self-defense of the Soup and Scoop, you poisoned Mr. Walburn's soup." Detective Lockheart cleared his throat and slid the piece of paper back to his side of the desk. "Chelsea Smith, a rival of yours, was just a happy coincidence, you might say."

"You think I tried to poison Chelsea, too?"

"The evidence is what the evidence is," Detective Lockheart recited.

I was getting very tired of his cold and calculated demeanor. "Are you arresting me?"

"Not at this time. We need to wait for the forensic results of the soup. But if the results are positive, then, yes, I do plan to arrest you."

I collapsed back into the hard wooden chair, my mouth agape.

"I'm telling you right now that you may not leave the town for any reason until the investigation is complete."

I must have sat there for a few moments opening and closing my mouth like an oxygen-starved fish. When I caught myself, I stopped and cleared my throat. "The results from the soup will prove that I didn't do it. I haven't poisoned anyone."

Detective Lockheart walked around his desk to my side. "Hire a lawyer. It's in your best interest. I'm sorry that things have come to this." He stood there for a long moment while I tried to process everything. I stood up and nodded my head, checked my back pocket for my cell phone, and left the police station.

I staggered up the street back toward my house, glancing over at the Soup and Scoop. Still empty and dark. I looked up the street to Aerie's house. I didn't feel like I could talk to her right now. The only thing I felt like doing right now was curling up under the covers and snuggling with Arnold and Ozzy.

I unlocked the front door and Ozzy jumped at my shins, and Arnold rubbed against the side of my leg.

My phone buzzed in my back pocket. I pulled it out and looked at the screen. Nothing. I had gotten rid of the notification screen. I thumbed in my password and noticed that my sister had texted. *"Where are you?"*

Where was I, indeed. I was in a nightmare; the main suspect of a murder, looking guiltier every time Detective Dan dug any deeper. I had to do something. I sat down on the floor in the dining room and stared at her text. But I still couldn't do it. I couldn't call my sister and ask for help.

6

Sitting in the middle of the dining room floor gave me direct access to Arnold's accusing golden glare. *You should ask Darla for help. She's very good at helping people.*

"I don't want Darla's help."

Even if that means the diner stays closed?

"It won't stay closed for long. I just need to figure out how to get around Detective Lockheart."

Okay just so you know I will say, "I told you so." When it doesn't work out. He paced in front of me making sure to drag his fluffy tail near my face. *And I'll repeat it often.*

"Thanks a lot, buddy."

Ozzy whined for a treat. I stood and opened the treat container and handed her one after she sat politely.

Arnold snuffled his distaste. *Dogs will do anything for food.*

"Here's one for you too, because I know even with your bravado you want some, too." I dropped a cat treat on the floor for him. "And because I know you won't get the chance to tell me you told me so." I only hoped I was right.

Even if I wouldn't ask for help from my sister, I knew I

could rely on Aerie. We'd done this whole thing before, after all. Only last time what was under the microscope had just been me, and not her entire business.

I headed over to Aerie's. I crossed the street and walked past the diner. Only a tiny sliver of neon green attached to a piece of tape remained on the front of the building. Chelsea had taken everything home. She was still a suspect on my list. I couldn't understand what Jay saw in her. To each his own, I guessed.

I knocked on Aerie's front door. I waited a minute without a response. I reached for the doorbell and pressed it and knocked again. I listened hard to hear if anyone was coming toward the door. What I heard wasn't footsteps arriving to let me in. It was loud voices. Aerie and Jay fighting. Screaming at each other, really. No wonder they couldn't hear the doorbell. For a moment I contemplated leaving them to it. But then I recalled my own sibling arguments. They could go on forever until someone stepped in to either separate us or talk some sense into us. I turned the front doorknob to see if it was open and it was. Ah, Aerie, so trusting.

I stepped inside. "Hey, guys. It's me," I announced. The yelling came from upstairs. Punctuated by a slamming door, which made me jump. I grinned. A slammed door was a good way to finish your argument. Like putting a gigantic exclamation point at the end. Jay pounded down the stairs carrying a small bag. He glanced at me but pointedly ignored me as he stepped around and out the front door.

Aerie stood at the top of the stairs with her hands on her hips. "And don't come back until you're dating someone nice."

The front door slammed shut. Another exclamation point. "Nice?" I asked Aerie.

45

"He makes me so mad. Nice was the first thing that came to my mind. It's the opposite of Chelsea."

"Was this fight with Jay about what Chelsea did this morning?"

"What Chelsea did this morning?"

"Oh, so you don't know how she plastered the front of the diner with skulls and crossbones?"

She ran down the stairs and pulled back the curtains on the front window. Angling her head at such an awkward angle I had to stop her.

"Don't worry, they're all gone. Detective Lockheart had her take everything down." Humor leaked into my voice when I thought of what it would have looked like from this angle if Aerie had been looking out her window at that moment. The almost cat-fight. I filled her in, pointing to my raw cheekbone.

"She hit you?" Aerie led me to the kitchen and gave me ice wrapped in a towel. I sank into a chair and put in on my face even though it was probably too late to do any good. But it did feel good to have my friend take care of me. I knew I could count on Aerie. I tried to push away the fact that she was still a suspect on my list.

Aerie dropped into a chair next to me and took a long deep breath. "*Om, shanti, shanti, shanti.*"

I looked at her questioningly. She took another deep breath in and out. "I'm practicing peace. If I am going to be the Mama Duck in your life, I need to focus on what is important and not the squabbles with my ill-guided brother."

She took one more deep breath in and out and her face relaxed into a genuine smile.

"So, how did Detective Lockheart know to be there this morning to break up the catfight?" By her tone, I could tell that she wished she could have been in that fight with Chelsea.

"Good question. He keeps showing up wherever I happen to be."

"Hmm. What do you mean?"

"Last night I went to the diner."

"Oh? Looking for clues? I could have helped. Next time, call me."

I couldn't tell her that the whole reason I went over to the diner was to prove to myself that she couldn't have had anything to do with it. "I wanted to walk around and remember everything that happened. But then Detective Lockheart showed up and read me the riot act and told me that he would arrest me if he saw me investigating the case again."

Aerie grinned and nodded.

"Why are you grinning?"

"No reason. Go on."

"Well, he made me mad and I went home. But then this morning I was out walking Ozzy really early; like five a.m. I looked over at the diner to see Chelsea taping skulls and crossbones on the front of the diner. So, I marched across the street to tell her off."

"I told you she had something to do with this. She wants to see the diner fail so that I lose the house and Jay has to move in with her permanently. He was here picking up more stuff."

"Well, you can thank her for hitting me, because that got Lockheart on my side, at least momentarily."

"I totally think he's on your side. No matter what he keeps saying." There was that smile again.

"He's definitely not on my side. In fact, he told me I'm the prime suspect of the murder investigation."

Aerie frowned. "Oh, no. Did he get the results back from the mushroom soup?"

"Not yet. But some review that Mr. Walburn wrote was found on his computer. It looks like he was going to bash my cooking."

"How would you know about a review on his computer if he hadn't published it yet?"

I shrugged. "Detective Lockheart still says it's pretty damning evidence and that I'm not allowed to leave town. So, pretty much we need to find out who did this and fast. Before Detective Lockheart puts me in a jail cell like he so desperately wants to."

My cell phone buzzed again. I didn't even bother to look at it this time.

"Aren't you going to get that?" Aerie seemed content to change the subject.

"It's my sister." I placed the phone on the table between us.

"Why won't you answer it?"

"It's complicated."

"Aren't all relationships?" She sighed. Clearly Jay was still on her mind.

"She's just going to yell at me about my poor decision-making skills. And if I were to mention anything about the ongoing investigation, she'd have a field day."

"You should still talk to her. I hate that Jay and I are fighting."

"You hate him dating Chelsea. That's why you guys are fighting."

"Well, that's true. I want him to date someone kind. Not that...bully."

"Chelsea's just milking this for all it's worth. But I think she's too self-absorbed to actually make herself sick just to manipulate your brother."

"Maybe she did it by accident." Aerie got up and put the kettle on the stove.

"I suppose that's a possibility, but there was something about her hitting me today that made me think she's not sneaky about getting what she wants. I don't think she's patient enough to walk through all the steps to shut down the Soup and Scoop."

"All right, I'll give you that. Planning out something like this would take time and brain space that, you're right, I don't think she has." Aerie put a cup of tea in front of me and sat back down with one of her own. I loved that she already knew me well enough to not even ask if I wanted it.

I blew on the tea and took a sip. It hit the spot. "You know Aerie, Jay really likes her. You know I'm not a fan of her myself, but if you want to have a better relationship with your brother maybe you need to take a closer look at Chelsea and see why he might like her." As soon as the words were out of my mouth, I couldn't believe it. I'd been ignoring my sister for the past two days, and here I was telling Aerie to be the bigger person in their sibling relationship.

"After what Chelsea put me through when we were kids, I don't need a closer look."

I nodded. That was fair. Time to get back to the real business at hand. "Let's start by taking a look at all the suspects. Even though we both feel like Chelsea should be number one, let's check out everybody else, too."

Aerie nodded. I opened up the notebook I brought over. "We have our list. The next person we would want to look into would be Mr. Belinsky, Mr. Walburn's friend. What do you know about him?"

"Not much. I think he works at the newspaper, too."

I wrote down *newspaper* next to his name. "I suppose that's the next step. Let's head over to the community center and ask some questions." I took a giant sip from my mug. "After we finish your delicious tea, of course."

THE PLEASANT POND Independent newspaper office sat in the basement of the community center. Six desks were situated in the far corner with very little natural light coming in from the one overhead window. Fluorescent lights created an intense artificial glow over everyone. Oddly, I noticed a scarlet macaw perched on a coatrack. Its food and water sat in small dishes on the corner of the empty desk nearby.

When Aerie and I walked in, we barely received notice from the office manager. She was busy fielding calls and scribbling notes on various papers scattered across the desk.

"Hi. We're wondering if you can help us." She didn't even look up.

A shout I couldn't decipher came from the one semi-enclosed office. I could only assume that was the editor-in-chief. The office manager grabbed a paper from her desk and ran it over to the office. She seemed to notice us on her way back. "What can I help you with?" Clearly, she wanted to quickly check us off her to-do list. She parked herself in her chair and grabbed her pen to jot something else down.

"We're wondering if we can talk with Mr. Belinsky." I scanned the room. Almost everyone was absorbed in their computers. The editor was reading the paper that the assistant had just given her and looked in no mood for conversation.

"We have a few questions for him."

"He's not here." She picked up the ringing phone. We had been dismissed.

A young guy at the back of the room got up to get water from the cooler. He saw me too. I walked over and Aerie followed.

The young guy leaned forward and whispered, "What do you want to know about Belinsky?"

I wondered how he had heard that from across the room, he must have been paying attention without seeming like it. Suspicious. "Hi, I'm Mira and this is Aerie."

I shook his hand. He had a firm grip.

"My name is Fred Lowry." He shook Aerie's hand as well. And that's when Aerie noticed the bird, completely distracted, she stared, looked back at me and mouthed, "What? Why?"

I shrugged and focused on Fred. "We just have a few questions for him about Mr. Walburn and if he knew of any enemies Mr. Walburn might have."

"Oh, he had enemies all right." That brought Aerie's attention back.

"Why do you say that?"

"You mean besides the fact that everybody wanted his job? Including Mr. Belinsky?"

"There's more than that?"

"Yeah, Walburn was a womanizer. A real jerk."

"Are there any women that you know of who might tell us more?"

"Any of the women here." He waved his arm to encompass the six desks and their occupants.

I raised an eyebrow. "I see." We would have to figure out how to tackle that can of worms but first I wanted to follow the more obvious path. "Who wanted his job?"

"You should ask who was supposed to get his job."

"Oh okay, who was supposed to get his job?"

"I was." He punctuated. "Walburn was grooming *me* to be his replacement. I had been studying. I had been taking online classes. I know how to write a proper review about food. But who gets the job? Belinsky. That jerk. He doesn't know paté from crudités. The only thing that guy eats are ballpark hot dogs and pizza from the sports bar."

Thinking the direct approach the best, and wanting to cut the diatribe short, because I was now hungry. "Did you kill Mr. Walburn?"

Aerie glared at me.

Frank took a step back. "Why would I do that? He was going to recommend me for his job and now that he's not here I don't have it."

"Okay, thanks for your help, Frank. Sorry about the job."

"Yeah, well, maybe it's time for me to move out of Pleasant Pond. This place sucks."

Aerie and I walked away. "Disgruntled worker."

"Definitely."

"You think he did it?"

"Probably not."

"He made a good point about interviewing the women who worked with Mr. Walburn." But after looking around the room I realized we weren't going to be able to do that. Everyone other than Frank seemed to be up to their eyes in work.

I could tell that Aerie saw the same thing. "Newspaper deadlines."

"We'll have to come back later."

"Now where?"

"I bet we'll find Mr. Belinsky at The Pizza Pub. It is lunchtime." I was also hungry for pizza.

I waited until the door to the office closed behind us to tell Aerie my next thoughts, in case Frank was still eavesdropping.

"If we're going to go to The Pizza Pub, let's formulate a plan."

"What do you mean?"

"While we're there we should interview Sam Andrews, the owner."

"You're right. He was at the Soup and Scoop the day of the murder."

"It would make sense for him to poison the guy that gave him such a bad review and do it at the restaurant of his competitor. Two birds; one stone, as they say."

"Not the kindest saying," said Aerie.

"Okay, I'll stay away from that one in the future." Aerie didn't blink at investigating a murder but didn't want to think of someone hitting two birds with one stone. I totally understood, animals were often more appealing than humans. I didn't know what I'd do without Arnold in my life. I continued down my train of thought. "So, Sam gets away with revenge on the guy that tried to ruin his career, *and* he handicaps the competitor, possibly sinking our own business."

"I know. Even when the results come back, we can't guarantee that people will return to the restaurant."

I immediately regretted mentioning anything about the diner's troubles. "People will come back, Aerie. They may not know me as well, but they do know you and you're a wonderful person. They'll come back."

"I hope you're right."

"I know I am. Should we get lunch at the pizza place?"

"I'm not hungry."

"Me neither," I lied. The thought of pizza made my

mouth water. With the diner closed my meals were mostly out of a bag, of chips. I shrugged, buying food from the competitor who might be killing people to put us out of business seemed a rather large betrayal. I let my stomach rumble.

7

J ust outside of town, we pulled into the parking lot of the strip mall that held The Pizza Pub.

Half of the strip mall was under construction.

"What are they building here?" Since I'd only been in Pleasant Pond a week, much of it was still new to me.

"I don't know. I didn't even know that they were expanding the strip mall."

"Should we talk to Belinsky first?"

"If he's in there."

"I have a good hunch he is. Frank pretty much spelled it out."

The Pizza Pub had six booths and a pick-up counter with a large old-school cash register on the corner of it. Oddly, the entire right wall looked similar to my kitchen entrance. Floor to ceiling construction plastic taped with a nonexistent wall behind it.

"I guess the construction includes this place. Now I really wonder what's going on."

Aerie pointed to Mr. Belinsky sitting in the corner downing a piece of folded pizza with ravenous intensity.

Either the pizza was really good, or Frank was right about Belinsky's lack of nuance with his tastebuds.

I walked right up to Belinsky's booth and slid onto the seat across from him. Aerie reluctantly joined me. Belinsky startled but smiled. "To what do I owe the honor of the company of you two lovely ladies?" He looked us both over, top to bottom.

He was just as much an obvious flirt as Mr. Walburn. It made me feel like I needed a shower.

"We want to ask you about Mr. Walburn."

"Who, Wally?

"You don't seem so upset about his passing."

He shrugged. "Stuff happens. None of us gets out of it alive."

"We heard you now have Mr. Walburn's job as food critic at the newspaper."

"You think I killed him to get that stupid job?"

"Did you?"

"Do you know how much that job pays?"

"Free food."

"This county doesn't have enough decent restaurants to make it worth my while."

"You seem to enjoy pizza."

"This? Sam's got the best pizza I've eaten since I lived in New York."

Okay, so secretly, I desperately wanted to try the pizza. But it felt like cheating on Aerie, so I quashed down the thought.

"Wally, he was a good guy. I don't really care about the job. I'm just going to miss a good friend."

He looked a little choked up before focusing on the pizza again, taking another bite.

"Well, thanks for talking with us, Mr. Belinsky." Aerie and I both got up.

"No problem, ladies." As much as I believed he was mourning the loss of his friend, I still had the feeling that he was scanning our bodies as we walked away. Yep, I did not like the guy.

Now we had to talk with Sam. We walked over to the counter. Sam worked in the back expertly pushing up the edges of the pizza crust then swirling the sauce. I watched, mesmerized. "Mr. Andrews?"

He looked up, surprised.

"We were wondering if we can ask you a couple of questions about what you saw the day of the murder at the Soup and Scoop."

He grabbed another pan with a ball of dough in the center and began stretching the dough out into a crust. "I'd like to help you out ladies, but I am very busy right now."

"We're just wondering why you happened to be at the Soup and Scoop on the day of the murder."

Aerie jumped in. "We know Mr. Walburn gave you a bad review."

Mr. Andrews continued to make the pizza and swirled pizza sauce around the second crust. "I've already spoken with Detective Lockheart. If you need information, I suggest you talk to him. Now really, I'm very busy today." He grabbed another pizza pan and started the process over again. "Unless you would like to order something, I suggest you leave."

"We're leaving."

I stormed out the front door with Aerie on my heels.

"Do you suddenly feel like maybe Mr. Walburn's skeezy friend didn't do it but that Mr. Andrew did?" I hopped into the driver's seat of my car.

"He was very evasive when we asked him questions." Aerie clicked her seatbelt.

"Yeah, it probably wouldn't hurt to find out what kind of construction is going on here." I let the car idle while it warmed up. My Buick was so old, it needed a little TLC before hitting the road.

"I'm sure we could find out more information about the construction by going to the town hall and asking whoever is on the planning board. They usually have to have a meeting to approve new construction in town."

"Oh my gosh. Duck." I grabbed Aerie's arm and pulled her down.

"What?"

"It's Detective Lockheart. If he sees me here, he'll probably arrest me."

"Dan won't arrest you."

"Oh, I can almost guarantee it."

There was a knock on the window. I straightened up in my seat and rolled down the window. "Hello, Detective Lockheart," I said in an extremely upbeat tone.

"Grabbing yourself a piece of pizza, Ms. Michaels?"

"Yeah. It was really good." I nodded emphatically, hoping he couldn't see through this blatant lie. My stomach growled in betrayal.

He gave me a look and then glanced over at Aerie in the passenger seat. "Good afternoon, Ms. McIntyre." Aerie let out a small squeak then cleared her throat. "Hi, Dan."

"I hope you ladies have a nice afternoon."

"Thanks, Detective Lockheart." I couldn't put the car in gear fast enough to get the heck out of there.

I pulled out of the parking lot at the speed of sound and headed back to town.

"He was just messing with us. On purpose." I felt my teeth grinding.

"At least he didn't arrest you." She giggled.

"I think he actually enjoyed that."

Aerie smiled to herself.

"What?" I asked, a little sharply.

"Nothing. I'm just wondering if Dan likes you."

"Absolutely not. That man drives me to deeper and deeper levels of anger each time he talks to me."

"I didn't say whether or not you liked him. I just said he likes you."

"Let's never have this conversation again."

That knowing grin played across her face again.

"And stop that crazy smiling. It makes me think you're up to no good."

"And what if I am?" She steepled her fingers and worked them together.

"One word, Aerie, one word. No."

Aerie shoulders dropped. "Okay, fine. You're no fun."

"Exactly, precisely. No fun. Stop having fun. Especially when it comes to Dan Lockheart."

My phone buzzed again. This time Aerie didn't notice, and I pretended like I hadn't noticed either. I dropped Aerie at her house.

I sat in my car once I parked in front of my house. Dan couldn't like me. He annoyed me every single time we talked. He was also overbearing. Always telling me what to do. Aerie was wrong, he couldn't like me. Nor would I want him to, I was happy to spend the evening with my furry companions. Maybe I'd splurge and order pizza.

8

My cell phone woke me at 5 a.m.. If my sister didn't stop calling, I was going to have to answer just to tell her to stop. I rolled over to push the button and silence the vibration when I noticed it wasn't my sister. It was Detective Lockheart.

"Hello?" My voice came out in a raspy choke.

"Ms. Michaels?"

"You called my phone, so yes, it's me." I realized a second too late that I shouldn't be flippant with Detective Lockheart if he was calling me at five in the morning. "Is there something wrong?"

"No. But I figured you would want to know the results as soon as possible. Your soup wasn't poisoned."

"I told you that."

"This doesn't completely exclude you from the suspect list. That review of Mr. Walburn's is still pretty damning."

"I suppose you wouldn't believe me if I told you I had no idea who he was prior to the day of his death?"

"It might, but that doesn't change how I will proceed with this investigation."

I rolled my eyes. Detective Lockheart was as by-the-book as he was grating on my last nerve, especially after hearing Aerie's thoughts about him yesterday. "Well, thank you for calling me at this ungodly hour. I do appreciate finding out that I didn't poison anyone with my soup." I couldn't help the sarcasm. It was early.

"Still, do not leave town until my investigation is complete."

"Understood."

"And no interference. I mean it."

"Also understood. Thank you, Detective Lockheart." I happily pressed the red hang-up button. I was still going to investigate. The Soup and Scoop continued to be under scrutiny. We needed to get our customers back.

I stretched and yawned. There was no way I was getting back to sleep now. I might as well join Aerie in her yoga class. Ozzy yipped, reminding me of my duties. I pulled on a pair of yoga pants and a tank top.

"Come on, girl." Ozzy raced me downstairs. I opened a can of cat food for Arnold, the click of the can bringing him running. "Early breakfast, buddy."

I'll eat breakfast whenever it appears.

"The early wakeup call was Detective Dan clearing me of poisoning people, so it's a win for both of us."

I grabbed Ozzy's leash and took her out for a quick walk.

BY THE TIME I arrived at Aerie's class, it was just about to start. I quickly grabbed a yoga mat, threw it on the floor, got into Mountain pose, and pretended to be relaxed while we breathed in and out. I opened my eyes to see Aerie giving me a weird nod and a shift in her eyes.

"What?" I mouthed silently.

"And we breathe in, bringing our heart up and open and breathe out, pulling our core to our spine, and again." During the pause she nodded her head in my direction. I shrugged to her. She'd have to be less obtuse this early in the morning.

"Over there!" she shouted and seemed to startle herself. She gave me a stern look, cleared her throat, and started again. "Breathe in, breathe out." I think she was saying it more to herself than anyone else in the room.

I giggled quietly. I had wanted something more obvious, but I still didn't understand what she wanted me to notice. She gave me a dark look. A look that meant more downward dog. After enough downward dogs to make my face turn purple, we finally ended class with Savasana. My favorite pose where all I had to do was lay on my back and breathe. I could totally do that, even before coffee.

While I had my eyes closed, someone nudged my shoulder. I blinked them open and saw Aerie staring down at me. "Mr. Walburn's wife is *over there*," she aggressively whispered while pointing.

On the other side of the room, which wasn't very large to start with, lay Mrs. Walburn, serenely enjoying her Savasana. I nodded, took a big breath in and settled back down on my mat. Aerie poked my shoulder again. Reluctantly, I sat up.

"You should talk to her."

"Can I finish my Savasana first? You ruined me with those downward dogs."

I heard that rumble in her throat, the one she'd mostly used on Jay when she was frustrated and/or angry. So, I got up, rolled up my mat, and walked to the back of the room to put it in the closet. I hung back while Aerie thanked everyone for attending and people idly chit-chatted their goodbyes. Mrs. Walburn headed for the door, and I slowly walked in her direction.

"Mrs. Walburn, I want to offer my condolences for your loss."

"Thank you."

"Detective Lockheart called me this morning to let me know that the soup was not poisoned. I don't know if that helps you."

"It does not. I was almost hoping it was an accidental poisoning with the soup. The wrong mushrooms or something."

"I understand." Aerie stepped to my side.

"I am terribly sorry."

"Thank you."

"Do you know of anyone that would want to poison your husband?"

"No. Who would want to do something like that? I was shocked when I heard. I came home as soon as I could."

"You weren't at home that day?"

"No. I was, um, visiting with my sister. Overnight, you know. We had things to discuss regarding our parents. It was quite a shock to hear about poor Eddie."

"Then you came home soon after you found out?"

"Of course. I went directly to the hospital. Later, Detective Lockheart asked me all of these questions. Are you working with him or something?"

Aerie and I both abruptly replied, "No." And blushed. Great detectives we made.

"I noticed you call him Eddie but Mr. Belinsky calls him Wally?"

"Yes, Gerard and Eddie were in school together, where he gave him the nickname of Wally, you know for Walburn. But to me, he was Eddie."

"We are both very sorry for your loss. If there's anything we can do, please let us know."

"Anything you ever want at the diner's free, on us."

Mrs. Walburn raised an eyebrow at that. "I'm sure you'll understand if I decline that offer."

"Yes, sorry."

I helped Aerie clean up the room after everyone else left yoga class. "Well, she was lying."

Aerie spritzed the mats with disinfectant and wiped them down. "Yeah, I thought so, too."

"Do you think she could really kill her husband?"

"I did read somewhere that women murderers like to use poison," Aerie said.

"What books are you reading?" Aerie reading books about poisoning surprised me. Or rather, she often surprised me, so why should I be shocked?

"Do you know where her sister lives?"

"I think she lives in Bloomsfield, but only because that's where her family is from. I'm guessing."

"I suppose we could look it up online to see what we find out." I led the way out of the rec building and Aerie locked up behind us.

"We get to open the diner today."

Aerie nodded but she looked stressed.

"Customers will come back, Aerie. I promise."

"Don't make promises that you can't keep, Mira."

"We'll figure it out. People will come if I have to stand outside handing out cupcakes."

She nodded. "Thanks. Come on, we have work to do."

Soup was out as a lunch option, at least for now. We highly doubted anyone would be willing to try the soup even though the mushroom soup was proved innocent of any wrongdoing. I doubted I would eat any soup made by me at this point.

We went through the morning prep like we usually do only this time there was a palpable level of stress. Aerie flipped the sign to open and unlocked the door. The line that usually formed outside each morning was not there. We weren't sure if anyone would walk through the doors today, or ever again. Jay wouldn't be coming in. He was still angry with us from our visit with Chelsea. Aerie looked so downhearted even I wanted to cry. "How about I make us some breakfast?"

"Sure." Aerie's response was barely a breath. She sat down on one of the counter stools.

"I'll cook you some of the new vegan bacon and that tofu scramble that you like."

"Sure."

I chopped mushrooms and onions and let them fry while I crumpled the tofu and mixed up the spices that miraculously transformed the bland tofu into tasting something like a southwestern omelet. It smelled so good I added some of the spice to my own two-egg omelet.

I pulled off strips of vegan bacon and laid them on the cast iron pan. I watched them carefully so they wouldn't burn. I knew Aerie could use some comfort food. I put her pan of bacon in the oven for a quick roast while I fried my own bacon. It was so quiet in the restaurant, when the timer went off Aerie jumped. I quickly plated everything and brought it out to the counter for her.

We ate silently. Occasionally I glanced at the diner entrance, but no one appeared.

"Maybe people don't even know we're open. We just need to get the word out."

Aerie nodded. She barely nibbled at her vegan scramble. But I did notice she enjoyed the faux bacon.

"We should tell Ellie." That was an inside joke. Ellie was the town gossip. She could spread news like wildfire.

Just then the bell over the diner door chimed. Old Mrs. Orsa walked in.

"You girls open today?"

Aerie hopped up with a bright smile on her face. "Absolutely. What can we get you?"

"A cup of coffee and I smelled those blueberry muffins; can I have one of those please?"

"Sure thing." Aerie rushed to the coffee pot and grabbed one of the heavy white diner mugs that I had slowly come to appreciate for keeping my coffee hot.

"Would you like your muffin toasted?"

"Yes, please, with butter."

"Will do."

Aerie bobbed into the kitchen wearing the brightest smile I'd seen in days. She only needed one customer to be happy. I snagged the dish of butter from the refrigerator and set it on the prep table for her. No one else came in for breakfast, just Mrs. Orsa. When she paid the bill, she tipped us an extra twenty bucks.

"I can't take this, Mrs. Orsa."

"I know you girls are having a hard time of it. You take that money and use it well."

"Thank you, Mrs. Orsa. We will."

"People will come. Don't you worry. It just takes time." She closed her purse and headed out the door.

I had cleaned the grill and was contemplating what we should eat for lunch while Aerie cleared away Mrs. Orsa's table. Today was already shaping up to be a long day. But then the door chimed again. Dan Lockheart walked in with his typical detective swagger and sat down at the counter.

Immediately, I thought about our conversation with Mrs. Walburn this morning and I rushed over. "I'm not investigating anybody," I lied. Better to lay down some groundwork in case he heard anything.

"Okay."

Aerie gave me a look and walked around the counter to face Detective Lockheart. "Can I help you with anything today, Dan?"

"Sure. What's today's lunch special?"

I looked at him. "Is that some kind of joke?"

"No."

"You seriously want to know what our specials are?"

"I'm hungry."

"Well, we don't have soup today."

"I figured as much."

"No specials today, just the usual." Aerie pointed to the menu pinched between the napkin holder and ketchup.

Detective Lockheart pulled out the menu, reviewed it quickly and put it back. "I'll have a hamburger with dill pickles and ketchup, with fries."

"Anything to drink?" Aerie asked.

"A glass of ice water is fine."

Aerie was as self-conscious as I was. She didn't bother putting the order on the board. She quietly filled a glass with ice and water, and I went back to the grill to start the burgers. I kept glancing at Detective Dan. He was up to something. Only I didn't know what.

Preoccupied by his phone, he didn't glance up once.

I dropped the fries into the fryer and set the timer.

Before I knew it, the burgers were done. I plated them on the bun, added dill pickle chips and the fries, and handed the plate to Aerie. She walked over to the counter carrying the plate with two hands, using extreme caution. She placed it ever so delicately in front of Detective Lockheart. "Here is your burger with dill pickle and fries." She gracefully picked up the ketchup bottle and placed it next to his plate. "And here's your ketchup."

The two of us stood behind the counter, arms folded, watching him eat. It didn't seem to bother him that we stared at him as he chewed his burger and dipped his fries in the ketchup. Quite the opposite. His stoic behavior while eating made me feel like he really was up to something. It's as if he could see right through the two of us and know that we had been talking to Mrs. Walburn this morning.

It felt like it took him eight years to finish that hamburger, but he finally popped the last bite in his mouth, along with the last swallow of ice water. The diner was so quiet the clink of the ice hitting the bottom of the glass almost echoed in the empty dining room.

"Thank you, ladies, for the excellent lunch."

"No problem Detective Lockheart."

"Have a good afternoon." He left a twenty on the table and walked out of the diner.

Once the door eased its way shut Aerie and I both took in a deep breath, one that we had been holding the entire time he ate his hamburger. "What is he up to?"

"You think he was just trying to freak us out?"

"Yes. He is mean enough to do that."

"It's almost two. I guess we should close up."

"It will be better tomorrow."

"I hope so. Because it definitely can't go on like this."

Aerie was right. We couldn't have another day like this where only two people came into the diner. Where no one trusted us. We had to find the killer and let people know we were open--with poison-less food.

9

It didn't take very long to clean up the diner and lock up.

"Do you know who I want to talk to?" I asked as I pulled the key from the door.

"Dan Lockheart just left here. He just finished giving you the evil stare. And already you're planning to do the one thing he doesn't want you to do. The one thing you could get arrested for?"

"You want to find the killer as bad as I do. I can see it."

"Yes."

"And you'll do it whether Dan Lockheart wants you to or not."

"Yes." She was resigned. She would come with me.

"I want to talk to Mr. Walburn's brother."

"That guy we saw with Mrs. Walburn at the hospital?"

"Yeah. Who else is going to know about the dirty laundry that's going on in his family?"

"I see where you're going. He'll know if the wife is trustworthy."

"Exactly. Who knows what information he might have?"

"All right, I'm in." Aerie tightened her ponytail.

"Perfect."

"I need to know, too. I want people to feel safe coming back to the diner."

"Do you have any idea where his brother works?"

"No. But I think I have an idea of who we could ask."

I had met Ellie Bracken early on when I first arrived here in town. She worked as the bank teller, was twenty-something, and a huge lover of gossip.

We headed out to meet with Ellie.

Walking into the foyer I could see her reading a book, the paperback kind, which surprised me. "Hi Ellie. A paperback?"

"Sure. There's something about holding a book and flipping through the pages that I like."

"I guess you heard about Mr. Walburn."

"Yeah." She looked at me sideways. "Was it your soup?"

"No. Can you please let everyone know that our soup is very safe for everyone to eat?"

"Yeah? I can do that. Just for you guys." She grinned conspiratorially.

"Hey Ellie, do you happen to know Mr. Walburn's brother, Terry?"

"No. I've seen them in here a couple times, but he uses the ATM more often. He keeps pretty much to himself."

"Do you know where he works?"

Ellie leaned over and whispered. "I could look it up for you but I'm pretty sure Mr. Meyer is currently watching and if he found out, I'd lose my job." She sat back. "I'm pretty sure he's gunning for that anyway."

"Okay, don't do anything to lose your job."

"But my friend Josie at the newspaper could probably tell you. She dated him. I totally told her to drop him." She shook her head.

"Josie at the newspaper?"

"Yeah, just tell her I sent you." She winked. "But promise me you'll let me know what you find out."

"Will do. Thanks Ellie."

"See you later. And good luck." She went back to her paperback, something called "The Surge".

WE WALKED across town to the newsroom. I wanted to find Josie quickly. The sooner we talked to the brother, the sooner we would figure this all out. We still needed to interview the women who worked with him to see if they could shed light on Mr. Walburn as well.

I stepped up to the office manager's desk. She was on the phone. She raised one finger for me to wait. Across the room the macaw sat on the desk delicately eating seed from one of the small dishes. When the office manager finished the phone call and hung up. It immediately rang again. She turned to us. "One minute."

She answered, "Pleasant Pond Independent, please hold." She pushed a button on the phone and hung up the receiver. She looked at us. "Can I help you?"

"Yes. We were wondering if you knew Josie. Ellie sent us."

She blinked and smiled. "I'm Josie." She stood.

"Oh." I thrust out my hand. "I'm Mira and this is Aerie." Aerie smiled.

"Nice to officially meet you. Ellie sent you?"

She was cordial but she glanced at the phone. She still had someone on hold on line I.

"Yes, Ellie said you might know Mr. Walburn's brother?"

"Oh, that jerk."

"Do you happen to know where he lives or where he works?"

"Yeah. I know where he works," she said bitterly. "And when you see the guy you tell him that Josie says he's a jerk."

I nodded my head. "Sure."

"On second thought don't tell him anything. He works for the town. Basic maintenance stuff. You know, mowing the lawn in the town center, cleaning the public pool in the summer, that sort of thing. He was a nice guy when we first met. But he always compared me to some ex and then he, like, totally ghosted me. The jerk."

"Do you know how we can get a hold of him?"

She let out a big sigh. Pulled open the bottom drawer of her desk and retrieved an address book. She flipped to the back of it. "Here's the phone number for the public works department. It'll get you to the dispatcher who can connect you with him. I deleted his personal number. Good riddance." She handed me the sticky note with the public works phone number on it.

"Thanks, Josie. We really appreciate your time."

She forced a smile. Obviously Walburn's brother was a sore spot for Josie. She picked up the phone. "Pleasant Pond Independent, thanks for holding."

Aerie and I had a phone number to call.

WE STOOD outside the diner in the bright light of late day.

"You're sure you're okay with this?" Aerie wielded the shovel like a pro.

"Do you really think this is going to work?" I looked up and down the street.

"The public works department has to fix stuff, right?"

"Yeah, I don't know if this is a good idea." All I needed was Dan to show up while we were damaging public property.

"Terry Walburn is the only person in the department. So, he'll be the one to do this job."

"What if he's out sick today?" I worried my fingers over my cell phone case.

"He'll come."

"How can you be so sure?"

"Gut feeling."

"Okay, but if he doesn't show up what then?"

"I fill the hole." Aerie dug the hole a little deeper. The crack in the pavement made it easier if not exactly easy to dig up the pothole she was busy creating on the side of the street near the diner. She dug; I called the town office.

The person on the line let me know that the pothole would be filled today, as soon as Terry got back from the custodial work at the high school.

We raced across to Aerie's house to ditch the shovel and get something cool to drink. Then we sat on her front stoop sipping instant lemonade waiting for Terry to show up.

Aerie sat comfortably close and leaned toward me. "So what's this thing with your sister?"

"What do you mean?"

"She's called a lot. You haven't answered the phone once."

"It's sort of complicated."

"We have time right now." She noticed my reluctance. "Come on, I'm bored. Entertain me."

"My sister has always looked out for me. Sometimes a little too much."

"Having someone who has your back is never a bad thing." She could understand that much because of her older brother Jay. But my situation had a wider crazier level of zaniness.

"Well, she's really successful and wants me to be the same. But her kind of successful."

"Hmm." Aerie nodded her head.

"She always tried to fix things. She refused to let me succeed or fail on my own. Moving here is my belated coming-of-age, independence, move."

"And she's calling to check up on you?"

"Yes. And right now, I don't want to share with her our current dilemma."

"Right." She nodded. "All the more reason to solve this."

"And get our customers back." We sat there in an awkward silence.

I had more to tell Aerie. I just didn't know how to phrase it. We both sat there sipping our lemonade. She knew I was holding back. Finally, I just blurted it out.

"My sister's a psychic. A famous one."

Aerie turned her whole body in my direction. "Who's your sister?"

"Darla Damien."

I watched as Aerie's eyes lit up. "I've read her books!"

"Exactly." I moped.

"Sorry, I don't mean to be so enthusiastic. But they are really good."

"You see what I'm up against."

"Uh, yeah." She sobered. "That's gotta be tough."

"What's worse is she knows when bad stuff is going down. That's when she calls me."

"Now I understand." She turned forward facing the street and nudged me shoulder to shoulder. "You didn't have to wait so long to share that with me."

I shrugged. "It never came up. It's hard to live up to the expectations of a famous sibling."

"I'm friends with you, not your sister." She grinned her evil grin. "Can I meet her?" She took a long sip of her drink. "Just kidding."

"Ha ha, funny joke. Well, now you know why I don't answer the phone."

"Okay but promise me that you will call her once we cleared this whole thing up."

"Why?"

"Because it hurts when your sibling won't talk to you."

"Aerie, I'm sorry about Jay. It's my fault we went to visit Chelsea in the hospital."

"No, I wanted to go too. I understand that I need to believe Jay knows what he's doing. And as you said, let him fail on his own."

"Don't let him hear you say that."

"Oh, I won't. But I think I'm going to make more of an effort to accept his choice even if I can't be super friendly with Chelsea. I will try not to provoke her."

"I'll do the same. No provoking Chelsea." We clinked our glasses together like we had just made a toast, then giggled into our glasses. The utility truck rumbled down Market Street toward us.

I stood up, leaving my drink on the stoop. "Here's our guy."

"Be subtle."

"Please. I don't think that's possible."

Aerie waved a hand and pointed to the pothole. Terry pulled the truck up along the curb in front of the diner. The scent of tar wafted from the back of the truck.

"Evening ladies. You got a pothole that needs filling?"

"Yes. It's right over there."

Terry opened the back of the truck and pulled out a long shovel. "How are you ladies doing this evening?"

He used the shovel to pull loose stones out of the hole.

"We're doing all right. We're sorry to hear about your brother."

"Yeah, heard it wasn't the soup. I guess you guys are open for business again?"

"We're trying to."

"Good luck with that." He leaned the shovel against the back of the truck and pulled out a bag of black asphalt that smelled strongly of tar. He used the shovel to slice open the bag and scoop out the wet looking gravel. It moved like black molasses. He threw a couple shovels full into the hole and put the shovel down against the truck. He reached into the bed again and pulled out a long steel pole with a flat end and began to tamp down the gravel.

If we didn't ask questions soon, he was going to finish this and leave.

"Terry, what do you think about your brother's friend Gerard Balinsky?"

A look of distaste crossed his face. "Never liked that guy. He's always wanted what my brother had. The job, the wife, he was always horning in on whatever my brother was doing."

"He was sitting with your brother during lunch the other day."

"Yeah. I know. They always had lunch together. I told the police, too."

"Do you think he did it?"

"He's sleeping with my brother's wife, isn't he?"

Terry pounded harder on the asphalt, flattening it against the roadway. He tamped it down a couple more times, and I couldn't help but think that he was imagining Gerard's face on the other side of that steel bar.

"I found out my sister-in-law is headed up to the Canyon this weekend with him." He shook his head like he couldn't believe it. "Eddie isn't even buried yet."

He pounded the ground a few more times. Once it met his approval, he threw the shovel in the back of the truck and laid the tamper next to it. Then he easily picked up the bag of stone and threw it into the back and closed the truck gate. He said nothing as he headed toward the driver's door. Aerie walked around the front. "Thanks for filling the hole, Terry."

"Sure." He started the truck and it spewed exhaust in my face as it pulled away.

I coughed and waved my hand in front of me. "I guess we should talk to Detective Lockheart."

"But maybe we could check out the Canyon."

I grinned. Aerie had a great mind for mischief. And she was right. The best way to prove Gerard Balinsky's motive would be to find him with the victim's wife.

10

_____

Aerie said the resort area of the Pennsylvania Grand Canyon wasn't very large. She said we should be able to find them easily, but after looking all morning, no luck. We had already asked at the two hotels in the vicinity and found nothing.

We sat in the outdoor dining area of a bed and breakfast that also served lunch. We were frustrated because the bed and breakfast also led us nowhere.

As we picked at our lunch, I watched as Aerie noticed how full the tiny luncheonette was. I knew she was thinking about the diner and whether we would ever get our customers back. I wanted to reassure her but right now I couldn't.

I forced myself to eat half of the club sandwich I had ordered. I had to admit the bacon on this was just right. But it was hard for me to enjoy it. I took a few sips of the lemonade. "We still have a few more places we can check."

Aerie nodded absently.

"Do you think Terry was lying?"

"I guess it's possible. But he couldn't know that we would come here and check."

"Exactly. He would assume we wouldn't verify one way or the other if his sister-in-law was here with Gerard."

"What motive would he have for lying?"

"His motive for lying would be if he was the murderer." I took another bite of my sandwich.

Aerie shivered. "I can't imagine any reason to kill your own brother."

"No. But then we," I waved a finger between the two of us, "are not psychopaths."

As I finished my sentence Aerie grabbed my arm and pressed it to the table. She froze and didn't say a thing. I turned slowly to look in the direction she was staring and I almost choked.

There they stood at the reservation desk waiting to be seated: Gerard and Nancy.

"They can't see us here."

"We need to get out of here."

I pulled two twenty-dollar bills from my phone case, more than enough for lunch, and placed them on our table. Both Aerie and I crouched and duck-walked our way to the back of the dining area. The lady's bathroom door opened, and a woman came out. Seeing us crouching on the floor she gave us a stern look and continued onto the patio. I pointed to the restroom and we hurried inside.

We stood and I checked the two stalls. Empty.

"Now what?"

"They can't find us here."

I mulled over what we should do. "Just seeing the two of them together up here at a bed and breakfast is pretty incriminating."

"But it's not evidence. Not of murder, anyway. Just an affair."

"True."

"We need to follow them to see if they do anything suspicious. But first we need to get out of here."

"Suspicious like what?"

"I dunno. Kiss?"

"I would assume that's going to happen at some point. Two people don't come up here to make funeral plans for their friend and husband."

"Good point."

"Okay, how do we leave without them seeing us?"

I looked up to the tiny window on the back wall. "Have you ever climbed out a bathroom window?" I asked.

Aerie shook her head no.

"Look at it as an advanced downward dog," I said.

"Ha, ha, very funny. Let's go."

I turned the latch and pushed hard. It wouldn't open. I had inadvertently locked it. It had been unlocked. "Ah, small towns."

"What?"

I turned the latch back and the window pushed open easily. "Nothing."

Aerie swung her legs out over the edge and jumped. I heard the crunch of branches as she landed in the low scrub brush that grew around the foundation of the building. She stood up and smiled. "Easy." She waved her arms for me to follow.

"Can you hold my phone?" I took my cell phone out of my back pocket and tossed it down to her. I didn't want to crush it when I sat on the sill to jump down. I leaned out the window. It was only five or six feet down, but I got a wave of vertigo. I did not like heights. I closed my eyes and took a deep breath. If Aerie could jump, I could jump. And I had to get the heck out of here before we got caught. I sat down on the sill and swung my legs out into the open and felt all my muscles go to jelly. If I sat here much longer, I would chicken out. I took another deep breath and pushed myself off the ledge. Of course, I could've told you what was going to happen; I landed hard on my left ankle and twisted it as I landed. I fell painfully over onto my side.

"Oh, my goodness, are you okay?"

"No." I hyperventilated. "I think I twisted my ankle."

It didn't quite hurt yet. That's how I knew it was bad. That shocky feeling that happens when you know you did something awful to yourself and knowing it would hurt horribly but you couldn't feel it yet. With apprehension I looked up to see a head peeking out of the window. "What are you two doing? Trying to get out of paying your bill?" It was one of the wait staff.

Aerie helped gather me up and we ran in hitches to the parking lot. Aerie helped me to the passenger side, and she ran around to the front. We peeled out of the parking lot, gravel spitting from our wheels as we sped out.

"I put forty dollars on that table," I shouted out the window.

"I'm sure they'll find it."

"I'm mad that they think we skipped out on the bill."

"I think you're mad that you sprained your ankle."

"Okay, yes that." I pulled up my pant leg and prodded at my ankle and flinched. The skin looked puffy, but it wasn't bruising. Not yet. My ankle began to throb.

"I'm taking you to the hospital."

"I just need some ice," I lied to myself.

"What you need is x-rays. I saw you land."

"Gracefully?"

"Hardly."

"We should follow Nancy and Gerard."

"Mmhm."

I took out my phone and looked up the nearest hospital in my map app, anyway. I gave Aerie the directions and said goodbye to our latest lead.

"I FEEL LIKE AN IDIOT." Aerie helped me limp into the emergency room.

"You jumped out of a window."

"You jumped too and didn't twist your ankle."

"I was just lucky."

"And I was just... oooh."

Aerie stepped up to the intake desk. "My friend sprained her ankle, we think."

I was handed a form to fill out and we settled in for a wait.

Aerie got up and dragged over another chair and picked up my foot and set it gently on the chair.

"Thanks, Mama Duck. I'm okay, really. If we just get an ice pack, we can be on our way. Then we can keep an eye on what Nancy and Gerard are doing."

"Right now, I'm going to bet they're finishing lunch."

"Okay right, but what about after?"

"I don't want to know what they're going to do after."

"Good point."

We sat for a while longer.

I broke the silence. "I suppose we'll need to share this information with Detective Lockheart.

"Yeah. He should know about it."

"Especially because I think Gerard is our man."

"You don't think Nancy could be in on it?"

"She seemed pretty sincere at yoga the other day. But she does have a motive, too."

"Not as good a motive as Gerard. Look, he's taken over Mr. Walburn's job, he's obviously also having an affair with Wally's wife, and Terry Walburn all but said Gerard has always envied Walburn's life."

Aerie nodded. "He was also sitting next to Walburn when he died. He could have given him something that poisoned him before coming to the diner."

"Exactly. We just need to find some incriminating evidence."

"Come to think of it, when I was taking their orders Gerard was pretty standoff-ish to Walburn. And then I noticed that Walburn started to flirt with Chelsea."

"I remember you said Chelsea flirted back."

"Yes, I'm trying to put that out of my mind so I don't stay angry with Jay, but whatever." Aerie shifted in her uncomfortable seat. "Yes, she was flirting with Walburn, too. He gave her a Lifesaver, and she licked it suggestively."

"Eww."

"See. I told you I was trying to put it out of my mind."

I flashed back to when I had absently started to clean up Chelsea's crumpled diner napkin. "I bet she spit it out. I bet all she did with that Lifesaver was lick it."

Aerie closed her eyes, like that would get the vision of Chelsea licking the Lifesaver out of her head, because it was in my head, too. "I bet the Lifesaver had the poison on it."

"That would explain why Chelsea got sick too. But not so sick she's six feet under. I might dislike Chelsea, but I wouldn't wish that fate on anyone."

"We found the murder weapon." I shifted in my excitement and pain shot up my leg. "Ow." I moaned at the deep ache in my ankle. "Well, at least this, I guess —" I waved at the offending body part —"was worth it."

"Gerard must have tampered with Walburn's pack of Lifesavers."

"And he just had to wait until after lunch when he'd have a mint."

"That's so calculated."

"He's sleeping with his best friend's wife. Which isn't exactly spontaneous or an accident. Terry was right, this guy really did want Walburn's life."

There was a flurry of activity near the doorway. EMTs brought in a gurney and we could hear them relay the patient's stats to the nurses.

"Possible poisoning."

Aerie and I perked up.

"Blood pressure is high, pulse is high."

"Okay, let's get him into room two."

We watched as they wheeled the gurney down the hallway. Moments later a weeping Nancy came through the doorway. She looked frantically around. "Where did they take him?"

A nurse stopped her. "He's in room two. But for right now we would like you to sit out here until we get him stable."

Nancy nodded with tears spilling down her cheeks, and headed in our direction. When she saw us she did a double-take.

"What are you doing here?"

"Sprained ankle," was my response.

She sat back into her chair dabbing her eyes with a tissue. And continued to eye us suspiciously. She took out her cell phone. She seemed to collect her emotions the more she sat there, texting. Aerie and I covertly watched her.

I took out my phone and texted Aerie. *Our theory just went down in flames.*

No kidding.

Do you think she did it?

Aerie shrugged as she thumbed in her response.

I guess it's possible. But now we need to know her motive.

Nancy glanced up and glared at both of us. It was almost as if she knew what we were texting to each other.

"The two of you were looking into the poisoning, weren't you?" she asked.

"You could say that. We want to let people in town know that our diner is a safe place to eat."

"Can I hire you?"

I stared back at her in disbelief, and then glanced over at Aerie whose mouth was hanging open.

"For what?"

"To find out who is poisoning the people I love." She sniffled and dabbed a tissue to her nose.

"Did Gerard just have a Lifesaver?"

"Yes," she looked shocked. "How did you know?"

"You know where the Lifesaver roll is?"

"No. Yes. I think it's back at the bed-and-breakfast. Maybe on our lunch table. Or in the room. Wait. I think he left them on the table."

A nurse came into the waiting area. "Mrs. Walburn, he is stable. You can come back now."

Nancy stuffed the tissue into her purse and stood up adjusting her pants and shirt. She started to walk away and then turned back. "You're hired. I'll pay you whatever you want." And she walked away.

Aerie beamed. "Do you think that makes us private investigators?"

I shifted in my seat and blanched as more pain shot up my leg. "I think it does."

"Do you think we'll find that roll of Lifesavers?"

"If we do, Detective Dan can't get on my case anymore."

"Not if we help him solve the mystery."

"If he was appreciative the first time we solved a mystery, he has a funny way of showing it."

WE CALLED the bed and breakfast as soon as Nancy was out of earshot. We convinced the hostess that it was of utmost importance that she search the trashcans at the patio dining area and Gerard's room for the Lifesaver roll. They either thought we were kidding, or didn't find anything, since when we called back thirty minutes later, they told us they found nothing. I suggested Aerie go and check to make sure, but she thought if either one of us showed up at another crime scene, it would get back to Dan and put us high on the suspect list. She had a point.

But every moment we waited in the emergency room brought us further away from catching the killer. We knew the murder weapon but didn't have any idea who poisoned the Lifesavers. We had no evidence that the Lifesavers were the murder weapons, and no suspects left.

I was finally called into the back to have x-rays done. After three hours, an Ace bandage, and crutches, I was more than ready to leave the emergency room. Nancy and Gerard had not reappeared. My guess was that they were keeping him overnight and Nancy was still with him.

"I guess it wouldn't make sense for us to go back to the bed and breakfast."

"Let's not become suspects again. You need to get off your foot, anyway."

I nodded. The extra strength pain reliever hadn't kicked in yet. We were only an hour away from home and it didn't make sense to add the expense of a hotel room on top of what I was about to be billed for the emergency room visit. I shivered at the thought. Now more than ever we needed to solve this murder.

I hobbled my way down the hallway toward the exit and almost ran directly into someone coming the other way. It was Detective Lockheart.

"What are you doing here?" We stared at each other.

"Sprained ankle. What are you doing here?"

He pointed a finger at me. "Stay away from the suspects. I will arrest you." He enunciated each word like I was hard of hearing.

"I don't know what you're talking about. Aerie and I came out here to sightsee and I sprained my ankle."

"You're telling me that it's just a coincidence you happen to be at the hospital at the same time as Gerard Balinsky? Who has just been poisoned?"

"Yep." Aerie nudged me with her elbow. I knew what she wanted me to tell the detective and I almost didn't want to do it. But it was in everyone's best interest for this case to be solved as soon as possible. It didn't matter who solved it.

"We found out that Gerard had a Lifesaver. We believe that's the murder weapon."

"I saw Chelsea and Mr. Walburn with them at the diner the day of his death," Aerie added.

Detective Lockheart looked like his head was about to

explode. His forehead grew red and his eyes were bulging out at us.

I put up my hands the best I could while balancing on crutches. "Look, don't have a conniption. This is what we found out and we're sharing it with you."

"Sharing it with me?" Detective Lockheart pointed his finger at me again, something I despised. "If I see you anywhere near this investigation again, I'm locking you up. I am not kidding."

"I'd like to see you try."

"Don't tempt me."

Aerie hooked her arm into my elbow. "We need to be going. Now." She tugged me forward and I almost tripped over the crutch I was leaning on. To keep from falling, I crutched my way out of the emergency room with Aerie attached to my side.

"You have to stop provoking him."

"Provoke him? He's the one who's pointing his finger in my face and yelling at me."

"You couldn't just give him the information and let it go?"

"Obviously not." I slouched in the car seat, my ankle aching, my head throbbing in anger, seething. Detective Lockheart got under my skin.

"We have no suspects."

Aerie focused on the road in front as she drove. But I could see her shoulders slouch. "If Mrs. Walburn is hiring us to find the killer, she can't be the murderer. If Gerard ate a Lifesaver, he can't be the murderer.

"Unless, he's either stupid or willing to get really sick so he won't get caught. There's no reason for him to do it out here. But then Detective Lockheart showed up. Why?"

"He probably has a friend at the Pine Creek police

station. And when someone called in the poisoning, they must've called him."

"Who else could it be?" I didn't want to think about it anymore. The whole situation was depressing. The diner was slowly sinking, my bills were multiplying and neither of us had any idea how to fix the situation.

Right now, I just wanted to get home and go to bed. I laid my head back against the headrest. "Hey Aerie, thanks."

"For what?"

"For taking me to the hospital. For just being here."

"You're welcome. Try to get some rest before we get home."

I closed my eyes. And my cell phone rang.

"You should answer the phone."

"It's my sister."

"She's worried about you."

"I know." I picked it up and texted her.

I'm okay. Really.

She texted back. *Talk to me.*

"What did she say?"

"She wants me to talk to her."

"Of course, she does. Why can't you?"

"I just..." How could I tell Aerie that I needed to have my act together before I could talk to my sister? Because right now I felt like a failure. "I just want to have this case solved first."

"Will you promise me you'll call her, like by voice, when we solve this case?"

"If we solve this case."

"WHEN. When we solve this case, because we will. We have to."

I closed my eyes for the rest of the way home. She was right. I had to solve this case. I owed Aerie that much.

She helped me into the house and got me settled in bed with a cup of water on the nightstand next to two extra-strength pain relievers.

"I'll be okay."

"I know. Get some rest, I'll walk Ozzy for you."

"We'll figure it out, Aerie, we'll get the diner back up and running."

"Get some sleep. I'll check on you tomorrow."

Aerie left looking hopeless. I laid my head back on the pillow and sighed. My ankle was now a dull ache that wouldn't go away.

Arnold hopped up on the bed. His delicate paws pushed down the comforter as he walked. *You smell bad. Where have you been?*

"In an emergency room getting x-rayed," I told him out loud.

What exactly is the process of getting x-rayed?

"X-rays are, well, they're these things, rays... oh never mind. I sprained my ankle."

Have you licked it?

"Humans don't lick injured body parts." Eww.

He turned in a semi-circle and snuggled down next to me. *I've missed you. I'm glad you're home. Now, don't snore.*

"I don't snore."

I beg to differ. He licked his front paw and put his head down on top of both his front paws.

"Good night, Arnold."

Good night.

THE NEXT MORNING, I woke up angry with my ankle feeling like a heavy weight that throbbed with each heartbeat. I realized most of the anger was directed at Detective Lockheart. It wasn't so much what he said, but how he said it. It had been like he was explaining to me how I was supposed to obey him. Which worked exactly like fingernails on a chalkboard.

He could have simply asked me to share my information with him or thanked me for the information that I did give him. But no, he pointed his big old finger in my face and reprimanded me like a child. I wasn't a child. I wouldn't let this investigation go. Aerie's livelihood, as well as mine, was at stake and there was no way I was leaving that all up to Detective Lockheart to set right.

My first thought was to meet Aerie at yoga this morning. I was hoping to talk to Nancy Walburn again to see if she had any clues as to who could be behind the poisoning. But I looked down at my thick, wrapped-up ankle and realized that was a no-go.

I gave up trying to put on yoga pants and settled for the baggiest sweats I owned. Nothing but sweatpants would pull on over my enlarged ankle with its bandage. I teetered along on the crutches taking twice as long to get ready as usual, and that was simply washing my face and brushing my teeth.

Arnold and Ozzy followed me downstairs where I fed them both and clumsily latched Ozzy's leash to her collar. "Okay girl, we're going out for a stand, instead of a walk."

While Ozzy sniffed and peed on the gate in front of the house, I called Aerie.

"How are you feeling?" was her answer.

"Like I fell out a window and wrecked my ankle. Hey, can you do me a favor and ask Nancy Walburn who she thinks might have done the poisoning?"

"Of course. I had planned on it."

This was important to Aerie, too. "I'd come to yoga, but..."

"I can give you some exercises to do at home. Get some rest. I'll let you know what I find out."

"Feel free to stop by after class. I'm not going anywhere."

"Sure thing."

By this point Ozzy had done her business. I had to credit my prior yoga classes for the level of balance I had to achieve in order to grasp one crutch and stoop down to do clean up.

While I waited to see what Aerie found out, I went back inside and treated myself to a bowl of Cap'n Crunch cereal and to make the new list of suspects.

I sat on my bed and elevated my ankle and thought. At first, I came up with nothing. So, I decided to simply list out everyone we came into contact with since we started this case. If the poison was in the Lifesavers, it could have been someone who wasn't even at the diner that morning.

The list included everyone at the newspaper where Mr. Walburn had worked, all of his family members, and I even kept Gerard's name on the list. He still had quite a motive and I couldn't exempt him from trying to avoid suspicion by making himself sick. About an hour later, I hobbled downstairs to open the door for Aerie. To my surprise, Nancy Walburn was with her.

"She says she'd like to help in any way she can." Aerie stepped into the house with Nancy behind her.

"The two of you have done such a great job with the diner, I hate knowing that all of this has impacted your business."

"And you'd like to find your husband's killer, too, right?" I asked.

She became flustered. "Well, of course."

I motioned for everyone to sit around my pathetic card table in the dining room. I offered beverages. Unsurprisingly, both passed on room temperature cans of ginger ale and tonic water.

Nancy took a deep breath. "It's obvious the two of you know of my relationship with Gerard."

We both agreed.

"We saw you together at the bed-and-breakfast restaurant," Aerie added.

"Where this happened." I pointed out my puffy ankle.

"Ed and I had been estranged for quite some time, you understand."

I was reminded of Aerie explaining how Mr. Walburn was flirting with Chelsea during the lunch and I nodded. "But you didn't want him out of the picture?"

"I didn't kill him, if that's what you're asking."

I nodded but watched her closely.

"I want you to find out who killed Ed and why they are targeting Gerard. He was lucky to get away with his life yesterday."

"Is he still in the hospital?" Aerie asked.

"No, but the doctor said he was very lucky that we got him to the emergency room in time."

"Can you think of anyone that would want both Ed and Gerard out of the picture?"

"I know things at the newspaper have been really stressful lately. Neither of them would talk about it."

I looked at Aerie. "Maybe we should head over there again?"

"Maybe *I* should." She gestured to my injured appendage.

"I'm coming with you. I might be slower, but I definitely

want to ask some questions. I elevated my foot all morning--it's feeling a bit better."

"I can pay both of you. Whatever you charge for investigating these things."

Aerie and I both looked at each other. "We aren't private investigators," I noted.

"We want to find the killer as badly as you do."

Nancy nodded. "Please, let me know if there's anything I can do to assist in the investigation. I need to know what's going on."

"We'll let you know what we find out." Aerie patted her arm. I tried to get up to see Nancy to the door, but Aerie waved me back and walked Nancy out herself.

After she left, I leaned over to Aerie. "Why do you think she's asking us to help and not asking detective Lockheart?"

"Maybe she feels like we have more at stake because of the diner?"

"She is also in your yoga class. Maybe that's just it. But I don't think I want to take her off the suspect list."

"Okay. She seems very sincere."

"I think I want a little more information on her before we presume her innocent."

"I'll ask around." Aerie picked up her yoga mat and headed to the door. "I'm going over to the diner and open it up."

"I'll come with you."

Aerie looked me up and down and gave me a questioning look. You can't stand all day on that ankle."

"I can sit on one of the stools. They are high enough for me to cook on the grill."

"I don't think you're going to need to cook. I'll be surprised if anyone shows up today."

11

I locked up the house and crutched my way toward Aerie, who patiently waited for me on the sidewalk. A quick glance down the street and we both saw Mrs. Orsa standing outside the entrance to the diner.

"Let me run down there and open it up for her so she doesn't have to stand."

"No problem. It will take me awhile anyway." Even the first few steps with the crutches and my armpits were getting friction burn. This was going to be a long day. But I was determined to make some progress in finding the killer. First, I had to get down to the diner without falling over myself on these crutches.

I watched as Aerie opened the diner for Mrs. Orsa. By the time I got there, Mrs. Orsa already had a cup of coffee and her morning muffin, another blueberry crumble.

"Oh, I heard you injured yourself. Does it hurt much?"

"Not too much. More of a hassle than anything." I smiled and lied. After the relatively short walk from my house to the diner, my ankle throbbed and I wished I had brought the pain killers with me.

I made my way over to the counter propped my crutches up against it and sat down on one of the celestial blue stools. The color alone was one of the reasons I loved this place so much.

Mrs. Orsa dabbed her lips with her napkin. "Soon as they catch the horrible person that did this, your diner will return to its usual business. People will come back. Don't you girls fret."

"Thanks, Mrs. Orsa."

The diner entrance bells jingled, and Ellie came in. She glanced around the empty room. "Wow, it's worse than I imagined." She saw the looks on our faces. "Sorry. Can I get a coffee and an egg sandwich?"

"Sure." Aerie turned to head into the kitchen.

I hopped off the stool and almost wiped out when I accidentally put weight on my right leg.

"I can do it." Aerie gave me a withering look and continued into the kitchen.

Ellie took my arm and sat me down on the stool. "I need to talk to you anyway." She pointed at my ankle. "What did you do?"

"Long story." But knowing Ellie, she'd want to hear about it sometime. "What did you want to talk about?" I leaned forward.

Ellie eagerly bounced into the seat next to mine.

"So, when I heard that the diner wasn't responsible for the poisoning, I immediately thought of Mrs. Walburn. Because we all know about her affair with Gerard. So, I looked up her bank statements." Ellie whispered the last sentence. "Always follow the money."

"You could get into a lot of trouble for that, Ellie."

She waved her hand at me. "Nobody except Mr. Meyer ever pays attention. Besides I'm doing it for a good cause."

She shifted on her stool and leaned closer. "It appears that Mrs. Walburn's business account, you know, for her makeup collection? Well, it's not doing very well. She has a small business loan out with the bank and it's overdue."

"Motive. If there's a life insurance policy," I said.

"There is."

"How do you know?"

"On the bank computers I can see the payments made to the insurance company."

Ellie was definitely a gold mine of information. "I figured you guys would want to know. Especially when Mrs. Orsa told me how bad business is right now because everybody thinks you poisoned some guy." She stood up when Aerie came out with the breakfast sandwich and the to-go cup of coffee. "The sooner you finger the murderer the sooner people will be back in here." She took the wrapped sandwich from Aerie. "But I know you guys didn't poison anyone. Besides, I'm too lazy to make breakfast." Ellie paid for her sandwich and coffee. "Thanks guys. Let me know what happens." As she left, she shouted over her shoulder, "See you tomorrow."

I shifted on the stool to turn towards Aerie who was behind the counter. "That's a good bit of information."

"It just occurred to me, if Gerard somehow found out that she murdered her husband, she could have purposely poisoned Gerard as well, so she wouldn't get caught." I propped myself up on the crutches. "She's definitely back on the list as a suspect."

"I just can't imagine that Nancy would kill her own husband."

"She did seem pretty sincere at my place. But she has motive, and she knows both men."

"So, we keep her on our list of suspects." Aerie absently wiped down the counter.

"I want to head over to the newspaper again and have another discussion with Josie. Just to cover all our bases." But also, because I couldn't go running to Detective Lockheart and tell him our information. I really did have to act like a private investigator and follow all the leads to narrow down the possible suspects.

"I can drive you over there. It's not like business is bustling."

"Thanks. But I might be a while. I'm thinking I'd like to interview all of the women at the newspaper who were harassed by Mr. Walburn."

"Let me help. It's better than sitting alone in the diner."

"Sure. The sooner we can wrap this up the better."

We waited until Mrs. Orsa finished her breakfast. And Aerie quickly cleaned up.

I managed to get my crutches wedged into the backseat of her car and hopscotched my way into the front seat and closed the door.

WHEN WE ARRIVED at the newspaper office, everyone was running around. It was even a greater level of chaos than we had seen before. I crutched up to Josie's desk, and asked, "What's going on?"

She furiously typed on her computer while trying to field calls. Finally, she glanced up. "Word from on high is we need to add an article about the new movie theater going in. And it's timely because they want to have a groundbreaking ceremony next week. Because of that, we need to shift everything in the newspaper to fit this thing. It's a nightmare." Josie answered the phone. "Paradise Pond Independent, please hold."

Something clicked into place. "Is the theater going in next to Sam's Pizza Pub?" I asked.

"Yeah, the construction is ready to start. I don't know why they didn't let us know about this ceremony sooner." She shook her head. "Sorry guys, I can't chat." She picked up the phone. "Paradise Pond Independent, can I help you?"

"So maybe that's why Sam is so stressed out?"

"I guess so. Which takes him off of our suspect list." Aerie grinned.

"Oh good. I want to try his pizza."

"We need to wait until things settle down here." Aerie took out her car keys.

"I suppose we should verify that Sam is no longer on our suspect list."

"You're hungry for pizza, aren't you?"

"Maybe it has something to do with my ankle?" I smiled sheepishly.

"You've wanted that pizza since the first time we set foot inside Sam's restaurant."

"The smell from the ovens in a pizzeria gets me every time."

"I didn't eat breakfast."

"Me neither."

"Do you think he's open?"

"It's almost eleven. By the time we drive over there..." I looked around the office once more. Everyone was much too busy to talk to us. "Let's go." In between calls, I caught Josie's attention. "When is a good time for us to come back?"

"Anytime after twelve-thirty." Josie reached to pick up the ringing phone again.

"Thanks." Although I doubted Josie heard me. Aerie and I headed to the car.

SAM FLIPPED over the open sign in the window just as we pulled up.

"It'll be a few minutes before I can get a pizza ready for you ladies."

"No problem, we have some time." Aerie smiled.

"We heard about the movie theater going in." I pointed to the duct taped plastic wall to our right.

"Yeah. And they're letting me put a door here that will lead right into the theater's ticket area."

"More business. Right?"

Sam's smile was infectious. "That's the truth. We can always use more business." He looked up from his pizza-making and acknowledged Aerie. "Sorry to hear about the diner. Has business picked up at all?"

"Not much or I wouldn't be here."

"We're hoping once we catch Mr. Walburn's killer people will realize we had nothing to do with it and will come back to the diner."

"You're on the hunt for a killer, are you?"

"Yes, just don't tell Detective Lockheart."

"He doesn't like you moving in on his business?" Sam smiled as he sprinkled cheese over the pizza sauce.

"That's an understatement," I said under my breath.

Sam chuckled. "You ladies want anything on this pizza?"

"Onions and mushrooms?" My favorite combination. I looked to Aerie to see if this was okay. She nodded. "We can put it on half. If you want anything else."

"Nope that sounds great." Aerie smiled at Sam.

We had a little bit of a wait while the pizza baked. Aerie took this opportunity to stand at the counter and talk with Sam about the restaurant business.

I sat, put my foot up in a booth, and looked at my phone. I hadn't heard from my sister yet today. I knew she was probably stewing in her own juices about calling me. She continued to ignore the fact that the whole reason that I came out here was to start my own life. On my own. Without her supervision, which was what my life had begun to feel like. Nothing was worse than having someone else micromanaging your life. I didn't think my sister understood that.

Still, I knew what Aerie meant when she said nothing was worse than radio silence from someone you cared about. I felt bad about not being able to answer the phone when Darla called. But I just had to get my life back on track before I could talk to her.

I looked up to see Sam holding the pizza peel and sliding the hot baked pie out of the oven. It smelled so fabulous and it wasn't even in front of me yet. My focus was now completely on Sam cutting the pizza into wedges. Aerie came back to sit down across from me and Sam brought the hot pan out to us and placed it on the pizza rack at the end of the table.

"This smells wonderful," I said to Sam.

"Thank you. I hope it tastes as good." Sam nodded.

"I'm sure it will." I picked up an ooey gooey slice from the pan and placed it on the paper plate that Aerie had put in front of me.

The pizza ended up being the most fantastic tasting pizza I had eaten in a very long time. Aerie and I both ooh-ed and aah-ed. Much to Sam's delight.

"Thank you, Sam, that was wonderful," I said as we were leaving.

"I'll see you later," Aerie added, and I gave her a sideways glance. She would have to tell me more in the car.

I hitched my way to the passenger seat and waited to hear the details.

"You'll see him later?"

"Oh, well, yeah." Aerie's smile gave her away. She focused on starting the car, but I recognized the guy currently walking into the pizza pub. It was Frank, the water cooler guy from the newspaper.

I pointed him out. "If he's going to lunch, the newspaper office must have calmed down."

"Let's go."

12

The newspaper office had calmed down considerably by the time we returned.

"Hey Josie, we're back."

The macaw suddenly let out a loud squawk, "The babe is back! The babe is back!"

I laughed. "Nice bird."

Josie squinted her eyes. "That bird is on my last nerve." She took a deep breath and turned back to us. "We finally got the paper out. With the substitution and everything. Now the world will know about the theater going in, like they don't already know when they drive by." She mumbled the last phrase under her breath.

"That's great, good job." Aerie cheered.

"That's the newspaper business. Crazy deadlines."

"We were wondering if we could talk with everyone here about Mr. Walburn. Do you think that's okay?"

Josie glanced in the direction of the editor's office. The editor herself was on the phone.

"Sure. The firestorm has ended, for now. We could all use a little break." The phone rang and Josie answered,

"Pleasant Pond Independent, how can I help you." She waved us toward the back of the room and pointed to a few of her colleagues. Aerie and I nodded and I crutched my way to the first desk.

"Do you mind if we talk to you about Mr. Walburn?"

The older woman clicked a few keys on her computer and looked up. "Sure. I'm Gloria. What do you need to know?"

"What was his attitude toward the women in the office?"

A woman I had seen in Aerie's yoga class named Sophia, joined us. "Mr. Walburn was kind of a jerk." Her glossy dark hair was pulled back, but a small braid was decorated at her temple.

"We are talking about the recently deceased? I'm Amelia, by the way." Her well-tanned bicep flexed as she pumped our hands. "Walburn thought we were his harem." She leaned back, put her hands in her khakis and snickered at what she thought was clearly absurd.

"Really?" I adjusted my crutches and leaned against the desk next to me. "How so?"

Gloria shook her head. "He was like a peacock with his hens. He would compliment each of us left and right and sideways. But then he would ask for a cup of coffee, like we were supposed to get it for him."

Aerie asked what I was thinking, "Did you get it for him?"

"No," the woman with the braid blurted out.

"Sometimes. If I was in a good mood, I'd get him a cup of coffee. Flattery can get you everywhere in my book." A younger woman with dark pink lipstick added. "I'm Mia." She put a well-manicured hand to her amply exposed décolletage."

"So, none of you felt like killing him?"

JULIA KOTY

"Mira!" Aerie was appalled at my question, but I knew she was thinking it, too.

Everyone laughed. "He wasn't worth any of our time. To tell you the truth." Gloria leaned back in her chair.

"If there was one person who really had issues with him, it was Frank." Amelia thumbed towards Frank's empty desk.

"But he told us that Walburn was going to recommend him for his job."

"Yeah, Walburn was grooming him for the job."

"Do you remember that time he actually was trying to help Frank get a date with Josie?" Mia feigned being aghast.

"I remember. That was weird." Gloria shook her head.

"Why was it weird?" I asked.

"It was weird because his brother was dating Josie at the time." Gloria shook her head like she would never understand his behavior.

Amelia leaned in with a wry grin. "You'd think the guy didn't like his own brother."

"What kind of relationship did Frank have with Walburn?" Aerie asked.

"It was more like daddy issues. He idolized the guy. So, if Walburn was in a bad mood and said something mean to Frank, Frank would pout for days."

"Do you think Frank could have done it?" Aerie asked.

"Nah, the kid is too wimpy. He loved the guy like a puppy," Amelia added.

"But you never know, do you?" Mia lowered her voice. "Do you remember that murder mystery on the mystery channel?"

Suddenly the conversation turned towards television mystery series, and Aerie and I ducked out.

"I kinda want to look in Frank's desk," I whispered. "You don't think anyone would mind, do you?"

Aerie glanced over at the group. "Frank is at lunch."

"As long as we don't take anything," I assured her.

We walked over to his desk. A quick glance across the top didn't reveal much, just a laptop and basic office supplies. I gently opened the top drawer. Inside I found a stack of letters that had Josie written on them with a heart as the dot over the "I". I picked them up and showed them to Aerie.

"Love letters?"

"Maybe." At this point Josie had started over to see what our progress had been. "Checking out Frank's desk?"

"We're just looking. We won't take anything." I hastily put back the stack of letters into the top drawer and started to close it.

Josie shrugged. "I don't care. Wait, what is that?" She must've seen her name.

"We think you have an admirer."

"Ugh. I told him months ago, I was not interested."

"I guess he still is."

"You can't turn off love." Aerie grinned.

"I don't want to know what you find in his desk." Josie threw her hands up and turned around to walk back to the front of the office.

Sophia's heels clicked across the floor as she walked over to join us. "What did you find?"

"Love letters to Josie."

"Oooh." Mia's eyes lit up.

I pulled open the next drawer and my mouth fell open. Aerie came over to look. Frank had a role of wintergreen Lifesavers sitting plain as day in the drawer.

"Don't touch it, that could be evidence," Aerie whispered.

"I won't."

"Evidence?" Sophia inquired.

"We think Walburn was poisoned by a tainted Lifesaver."

"Walburn used to eat those things like crazy. I hated the smell. Every day." Mia rolled her eyes.

"I suppose we need to share this with Detective Lockheart," I said.

"Yep," Aerie agreed. "I dare you to do it."

"I'm not doing it."

"We'll both tell him."

"Thanks everybody for your help." I thanked everyone.

As we walked past Josie's desk, she stopped us. "You found something else, didn't you?"

"Just a role of Lifesavers. But it could mean something."

"He could be the killer?"

"We don't know, we would need Detective Lockheart to have the Lifesavers tested."

Josie began to pack up her purse. "I'm going for something to eat. I don't want to see him when he comes back from lunch. Love letters and poison," she grumbled and walked into the editor's office. Aerie and I took this as our cue to leave.

Once I got my crutches jammed into the back of Aerie's car, I asked her, "Do you think he did it?"

"The Lifesavers are a pretty big deal."

"I'm just not sure of the motive. I mean if Walburn was going to recommend him for the job and even goes to the extreme of helping Frank get a date with Josie. It just doesn't sound like somebody that you would want to bump off."

"I still think we should tell Detective Lockheart," I said.

"And hope that he doesn't arrest us."

NOT A SURPRISE, there was no lunch crowd to greet us when we drove up to the diner.

After unlocking the door and turning over the welcome sign, I parked myself on my new favorite stool and took the weight off my angry ankle.

Aerie began to pace back and forth. "Okay, promise you won't get mad at me," she pleaded, "but when I was talking with Sam, he thought that maybe..." She walked over to me and sat down on the next stool. "Maybe it would be an idea, just an idea, that I let people know that I'm cooking at the diner." Her eyes searched my face.

"Okay."

"I don't like the idea. You're a much better cook than I am. But he said that there's not much I could do except wait it out, or I could say that you aren't cooking, for the time being, and maybe people would come back." Her eyes searched my face.

"Okay."

"You're not mad?"

"Aerie, I'm not mad. I have a busted ankle. I could barely cook anyway. I think it's a good idea."

"You're really okay with it?"

"I'm really okay with it." And I was. My ankle throbbed nonstop and balancing on these crutches was its own kind of torture. I felt horrible that the business had gotten this bad so quickly.

Aerie busied herself behind the counter in the kitchen. She was putting food into some grocery bags.

"What are those?"

"Some of the fresh produce that was delivered. I'm taking it over to the food bank. We won't be able to use it before it goes bad."

"I wish I could be of more help."

"Just keep looking for the murderer. I'll help as much as I can. The sooner we find them the better."

The bells rang over the diner entrance. Frank, of all people, walked in and sat down at the counter next to me.

"Hey." He sounded dejected.

"Good afternoon, Frank. How's it going?"

"Man, life sucks. Can I get a chocolate malt?"

"Sure." Aerie went over to the ice cream counter and scooped chocolate ice cream into the stainless-steel blender cup.

"Didn't we just see you at the Pizza Pub? They don't have milkshakes there?"

"I had a milkshake there, too. Dude, I try to be nice and all I get is flack."

"Really?" I needed Frank to open up and talk about what was going on.

"Yeah, I asked Josie on a date. Does she want to go on the date? No. But she just doesn't turn me down politely. No, she has to shout it out to the whole office, making me look like a complete idiot."

"So you're having the second chocolate malt of the day."

"Yeah, yours are better anyway. I'm done with Pleasant Pond."

"I'm sorry to hear that."

"I suppose you have to know when to quit. And I know now is the time to quit."

Aerie set down the thick chocolate malted in front of Frank who tore open his straw and jammed it into the frothy dark sweetness.

"I'll leave you to your chocolate. Hope it helps."

I hopped off the stool and crutched my way into the kitchen.

"What do you think?"

"I don't know. Seems like a sad kid."

"I nodded. "Yeah.""

I slowly helped Aerie pack up more of the produce that was headed to the food bank while Frank finished up his chocolate malted, alone with his thoughts.

Before Frank left, I wanted to ask him a question just to see what his response would be.

I came out from the kitchen as Frank was slurping his last sip of chocolate malted. He pulled out his wallet and took a five-dollar bill and put it on the counter. "Thanks. Didn't really cheer me up, but it tasted good."

"You're welcome. Hey, Frank, I have a quick question for you. Do you like wintergreen Lifesavers?"

I watched him closely. His expression didn't change. "Not really. You know, Walburn ate them constantly. It was like his thing, you know. I thought maybe if I ate them, too, it would be my thing. But that was stupid, they numbed my tongue and tasted like crap."

"Thanks for stopping by, Frank. We appreciate it. And I hope your day goes better."

"Yeah. See you." He pushed open the diner door and disappeared around the corner.

I watched him go and then hustled back into the kitchen. "I don't think he did it."

"How come?"

"Because he said he tried the Lifesavers because Walburn used to eat them all the time. It sounds like he thought it was his secret to success."

"That's dumb. Because it certainly was his downfall." Aerie picked up the grocery bags and lined them up on the counter.

"We're back to zero suspects again, aren't we?"

"No. Not quite. I think we need to check out Nancy's alibi

that she was at her sister's and see what we can find out about her makeup business."

"Is it okay if I sit this one out? I need to take these over to the food bank."

"Absolutely, don't worry about it. My ankle has been feeling a little better lately." I crutched my way to the front door and pushed it open and stood there like a doorstop so Aerie could bring the bags out to her car. "Do you know where Nancy's sister lives?"

"No, but you could ask Nancy. She did say she wants to find the killer."

"You're right. I think I want to ask her in person and see how she reacts to the idea of me talking with her sister. She could incriminate herself. I'll ask her to meet me at my house in an hour. And we'll see how it goes."

"Keep me posted. Because this whole situation is getting old."

"I hear you."

13

I shook Nancy's hand. "Thanks for coming to meet me today. I just have a few questions."

"No problem. Anything I can do to help." Her styled hair and makeup were a startling contrast to the sweats and t-shirt I was wearing.

"How's Gerard doing?" I offered her the other folding chair.

"Much better, thank you for asking." She sat and put her purse on the card table.

"You mentioned that you weren't home the day before Ed was killed."

"That's right, I was at my sister's. We were discussing our parents' living wills. Not a great topic. But something that had to be done."

"I'd like to meet and talk to your sister."

"What for?" Concern showed on her face.

"She might be able to shed some light on what happened."

"I don't understand why. She lives in a different town.

She didn't talk to my husband very often, except at family functions. I don't see why you need to talk to her."

"Let's just say I'm checking all my bases. You never know where some information can be hiding."

"She's a very, very private person. I don't think she'll like the invasion of her privacy."

"I understand. But if you could share with me her phone number, I would really like to talk to her."

I watched the argument play across Nancy's face. But then she surrendered. She reached into her purse and pulled out her phone. "Here's her number. But I don't think you're going to learn anything from her."

"It's okay. It's just something I need to do. I won't take up much of her time." After getting the number, I stood up on my crutches. "Thanks Nancy, for coming by today and letting me have your sister's information. I'll keep in touch and let you know what I find out."

"I don't think she has anything that will be helpful, but good luck."

Once Nancy was safely out the door, I texted Aerie.

She was very resistant to giving me her sister's information.

My phone pinged immediately.

You need to get back to the diner, ASAP.

Oh boy. What was going on now? More issues with Chelsea? I threw on my hoodie, not so much for warmth as for some padding against my armpits from the stupid crutches. And I made my slow, agonizing way down to the diner.

When I arrived the only person there was Detective Lockheart, sitting at the counter looking to have finished what appeared to be a hamburger and French fries. It was kind of him to come to the diner and have lunch each day. Still, the vibe was not a happy one. Especially when his eyes locked on mine.

He took his napkin and wiped his lips firmly. He turned to face me. "Thank you, Mira, for coming. Please sit." Already he was telling me what to do. And already I was getting angry. But my ankle was sore, and I wanted to get off these crutches, so I sat at the table nearest the counter. Detective Lockheart grinned as I did so, and I almost wanted to get back up on the crutches just to be contrary.

"Aerie, if you don't mind." He waved his hand at the empty seat across from me. "I understand that the two of you are very invested in the results of this investigation."

"Of course, we are. Look at this place. No one has come into the diner since you declared that it must be the mushroom soup. Which it was not. And now we have no customers." I took a breath noticing that Aerie was shooting me daggers quietly across the table. I breathed in slowly and exhaled slowly. I had to keep my temper. I had promised her.

Detective Lockheart simply nodded. "Yes, you're proving my point. Josie Colts came to me asking how she could get a restraining order on Frank Lowery. Do either of you know anything about this?"

I knew from the way he asked he already knew that we had been at the newspaper yesterday.

"A restraining order?" was the only thing I said.

"Yes, a restraining order. She feels unsafe in the newspaper office after *someone* found a role of wintergreen Lifesavers in his desk alongside a stack of love letters. And I know that someone was you, Mira Michaels."

I sat there and shifted my seat in the chair. There was

nothing I could say. I hadn't expected Josie to go off the deep end and talk to the police. I suppose if I was her, I would've done the same thing.

"I understand the both of you are highly invested. But I cannot, and I stress this, I cannot have either of you looking into this case while it's still under investigation."

Aerie and I both nodded.

"No. I don't think you understand. I have you both here so that I can be very clear. I will arrest either of you, or both of you, if I see you anywhere, and I do mean anywhere near any of the suspects."

I struggled to stand, leaning on the table and the chair which wobbled precariously under my grasp. "Look, Detective, if you were able to do your job faster, we wouldn't have to do any kind of investigating. But seeing as you still haven't found the murderer, we feel we need to do what we need to do."

"Let me repeat myself. I will arrest you. You will be placed in the jail cell in the basement of the police station. I cannot be more clear about this." He grabbed his jacket from the stool near the counter, pocketed his cell phone and made his way to the door before either of us could reply. "Have a good day, ladies."

"Well, now what?"

"We let Detective Lockheart do his job," Aerie said.

"But I have a lead, Nancy's sister."

"I've known Dan since I was a kid. I'm actually shocked he hasn't arrested us already."

"I can't just sit around." My brain raced through all the possibilities of suspects. I felt like we were close to finding the murderer.

"The universe has sprained your ankle for you. You need to sit this out," Aerie implored.

"Sprained ankle has nothing to do with the universe. You're sounding like my sister."

"Who you should probably call." She reminded.

"I'm not calling her until we've solved the murder."

"We are not solving the murder. Detective Lockheart is solving the murder. Please, leave it alone."

"But the diner..."

"The diner will be okay. For now. It's not going to help if you get arrested." The tone of Aerie's voice was something I hadn't heard before. She was upset with me.

But I couldn't let it go. I just had to make sure that the detective didn't find out. And now I just wouldn't be able to tell Aerie either. Because it would just upset her.

"Okay, look. I'll prop up my ankle and stay home if you promise me you won't give up."

"Promise you'll stay home."

"Promise." I wasn't lying. I had Nancy's sister's phone number after all.

Nancy's sister's name was Erin Walton. I settled into the brown lounge chair that Aerie had helped me find at a yard sale last week. It allowed me to prop up my sore ankle. Arnold hopped up a second later and quietly curled up in my lap and tucked his paws under and relaxed.

I put the number into my cell phone, took a deep breath, and pushed Call.

"Hello?"

"Hello, is this Erin Walton?"

"Yes, can I ask who is calling?"

"Sure. My name is Mira Michaels and I live in Pleasant

Pond. Your brother-in-law ... um, died in my diner. I wanted to let you know I am very sorry for your loss."

"No great loss to me. Don't waste your breath."

I wasn't quite sure what to say to that.

"You're still looking into who killed Ed, aren't you?"

"We are." My phone beeped. My sister was calling. I tapped 'do not disturb' on my phone and tried to remember what I was saying. "We're still looking. We would like to open the diner to customers again, but I don't think anyone will come until we've pointed out who did the deed."

"Hmm, I understand. Well, as much as you would think Nancy and Gerard would have reasons to do this, I think you should look into Ed's brother."

"Oh, why is that?"

"Every family gathering I went to, Terry was exceptionally creepy around my sister."

My sister beeped in again, this time with a text. *Call me!!*

Arnold noticed my sigh, stood up on my thighs and stretched, digging his sharp claws, that I forgot to clip, into my leg. I squirmed and tried to push him off.

"I understand you didn't care for Ed Walburn?"

"No. And neither did my sister, at least not for the last four years."

"Why didn't they divorce?"

"Oh, who knows. I think she was using him for the money."

"He works at the newspaper, doesn't he?" I knew most newspaper jobs paid notoriously low.

"Oh, Ed came from money. As long as he kept a job, he was entitled to a stipend from the family fortune."

"So, you're telling me both Terry and Ed are wealthy?"

"Yes, but Nancy was tired of dealing with Ed's

philandering. She couldn't care less about the money at this point."

"Although now that Ed has died, as his widow, wouldn't she get some of the money?"

"Nope, not a penny. And she doesn't want it either. She's been in love with Gerard for a long time. I expect they'll get married now. After things have settled."

"Does Gerard have money?"

"No, I don't think so. But Nancy has her business, and she says it's doing quite well. So, I assume they will live off of her earnings."

I nodded and said nothing about the overdue loan Nancy had taken to save her business. One sister keeping secrets from the other? Something I was all too familiar with.

"Well Erin, I thank you for helping me out today.

"Sure, no problem."

I ended the call. So, Terry was creepy, and Nancy was definitely lying about her money problems.

Nancy just became the number one suspect on my list. But then why would she ask for our help in finding the killer? Unless she wanted to feed us false leads.

Darla rang my phone again. I pushed decline. And immediately texted her back:

I'm busy. I'll call you later.

I highly doubt that. You need to know about a premonition.

I don't have time for your premonitions right now. I'm really busy.

I had a dream that you were trapped in a small room with no way out. So stop whatever you're doing right now. The path you're on is going to lead you there.

Can you just let me follow my own path without getting in the way?

I sent the text and tossed my phone onto the table. It buzzed one last time, but I didn't care what she said.

Arnold rubbed his chin against the chair. *You should listen to Darla.*

"You don't even know what she texted."

I know whatever it is made you mad and that means it's probably something you know is true.

"Oh, hush you. And thanks a lot for the claw marks." I rubbed my leg. "See if you get treats later."

I will.

That cat. "Don't think I haven't forgotten about the kittens."

Oh, Paternity gifts?

"Hardly. You'll be lucky if I don't have to start buying the generic cat food to make up for the cash I'm out because of your philandering."

14

Great. Now my sister thinks I'm going to end up trapped somewhere. Just great. I tried to blow it off, but my sister's premonitions were almost always spot-on.

There was only one way to figure out who the murderer was, and that was to trace the poison to them. Gerard was still a suspect, even if only slightly. Nancy was a suspect in a big way, so I couldn't ask either of them. The doctor in the ER wouldn't share that information, and I definitely couldn't ask Detective Lockheart what type of poison was used. Then it came to me. I called Aerie.

"Aerie? I know what we need to solve the crime."

"What?"

"We need to find out what kind of poison was used on the Lifesavers."

"I told you--you're going to get arrested. Leave this to Dan."

"No, we can't do that, and we can't ask Nancy or Gerard or the doctor that treated him. So, if we can't ask them, there's only one person we can ask."

"Oh no. Nope." Aerie said resolutely.

"We have to do it."

"Who says we have to do it? Just tell Dan and be done with it. I don't want anything to do with her."

"We have to ask Chelsea."

"I can't do it. Why do you need to know?"

"I've been sitting here mulling things over in my head and then realized that if we understood what poison was used, it might point to who the killer is. Because right now we just have circumstantial evidence and motive we don't have anything that points to the real killer."

"So, you want me to ask Chelsea to find out what her doctor said poisoned her."

"Yes. You can do it."

"Why can't you do it?"

"Because I bet you could make this look like you were coming to make amends with Chelsea. Jay would like that, wouldn't he?"

"But I'm not going to make amends with Chelsea."

"You can't hate her forever. She has some personality flaws, I agree. Her right hook was weak. The bruise on my cheek healed within two days."

"Ha ha. You even hate her."

"I'm not best friends with her, I have to admit. But she can help us with this investigation. You can't ignore that."

"Fine."

"You'll go ask her?"

"I still can't see why you can't do it."

"I'm injured. Good luck."

"You owe me."

TWO HOURS later Aerie texted me: *Rat poison*.

I texted back: *Darn, very generic.*

I would have to trace it back to where it came from. Either Nancy has some at her home, which she could have disposed of. Or I could check the municipal supply shed.

This meant I had to leave the house, and it also meant I definitely couldn't tell Aerie. I swore to her that I wouldn't investigate. But there was no way she would do it so that left me.

"Arnold. Cover for me. I'm heading out soon, watch the dog." I googled "how to pick a lock." It was time to learn some new skills.

15

I was here on a hunch. In the dark. I shook my head. Only I could get into this much trouble by following my hunches. Darla would remind me that it's called intuition, and that she follows hers like the Holy Ghost. But every time I follow my gut, craziness ensues. Like, right now, I was crouched behind the municipal supply shed. On the other side of the trees to my right was the police station. Of course.

But I needed to see for myself what my brain had been trying to figure out over the last couple days.

There was something to be said for being forced to sit still and think. My busted ankle forced me to sit and focus on the suspects and who they are and their jobs. And now my ankle felt better, and I reasoned out some logical answers about the murder.

This was why I was at the municipal shed. Because Walburn's brother works for the town, he'd have access to this shed and I'd bet dollars to donuts that somewhere inside this shed I would find the poison that killed Ed

Walburn and inadvertently, at least with Chelsea, had made others sick.

I still wasn't sure how to prove that Terry was our killer. But I was sure of it. Well, almost sure of it. I just had to get inside the shed and find the poison.

I wish I had Aerie here, but I promised her I wouldn't investigate. Prior to this expedition I had watched a YouTube video on how to pick a lock. I couldn't really practice on my home locks; all but my front door were old timey skeleton key locks. My front door faced Market Street, which was pretty obviously facing town. I couldn't sit there and pick my own lock in front of all the nosey neighbors who might be walking by. So yeah, this was my first go at it. It is funny what ex-boyfriends leave behind. The lock picking set was in my back pocket, the small thin set was the size of a credit card.

I was all-in. All or nothing. I repeated tiny prayers under my breath that this would work. But there was something odd about asking God to help you break into a town building, break into anywhere, really. I even looked up the patron saint of locksmiths. And I asked St. Baldomerus to nudge me in the right direction. I looked closely at the generic tumbler lock that secured the supply shed. I could do this. I grabbed the handle and turned. Locked. Hey, it was worth a try.

Breathe in. Breathe out. I pulled the little credit card shape from my back pocket and slid out the tension wrench and held it in my hand. It was a thin Z-shape piece of metal. Breathe in, breathe out. I inserted the tension wrench into the lock, then I took out the pick which looked exactly like its name and then dropped it into the grass. "Dang it." I reached down and had to feel in the grass for it because it was too dark to see. I wasn't about to turn on the flashlight from my phone. I found it quicker than I expected. This time I held the pick more deliberately and I inserted it into the lock. Breathe in. Breathe out. The moment of truth.

The video called this "scrubbing". I had to line up all the pins. "Okay, St. Baldo wish me luck," I whispered under my breath. I scrubbed the pin in the lock while at the same time I put pressure on the tension wrench. Scrub, scrub, scrub, tension release, tension release. Nothing happened. I mean I think I was getting some of the pins to line up, but not enough to turn the lock. I pulled the tension wrench and the pick from the lock and shook out my arms and took a deep breath. I could do this. I just had to relax. I tried again. First the tension wrench then the pick, and scrub with the pick. Release the tension with the wrench. Scrub, tension, scrub, tension, and suddenly, the lock turned.

"Yes!" I looked around and prayed that no one heard me. I dropped the pick again and fumbled to pick it up and jammed both pieces into my back pocket. Quietly, I opened the door and slid inside.

The room smelled of fertilizer and pool cleaner, and my eyes struggled to adjust. I could see the outline of shelving along the walls with a wide enough walkway for the trolley to carry the heavy mulch bags or blacktop bags like I remember Terry bringing to fill the pothole.

I walked deeper into the shed and further away from the doorway where the streetlight gave me some ability to see. What was I looking for? It wasn't like the poison would be on a pedestal with neon lit arrows pointing to it. Although that would've been nice. The further I walked the more claustrophobic I felt. And the warning from my sister banged around inside my head. *I saw you trapped in a small room.*

The light from the doorway was suddenly cut off.

Darkness closed around me. I heard footsteps coming in my direction. I panicked and tried to hide behind one of the shelves and tripped into it. Stupid ankle. And then my phone vibrated in my pocket. Why hadn't I just turned it off? It was my sister; I just knew it was. Leave it to her to mess things up.

"I know you're in here." The voice of Detective Lockheart. The bane of my existence. I couldn't hide in an eight by ten shed.

I stepped out from behind the shelf and faced my nemesis. "Detective Lockheart."

"I should have known it was you." Detective Lockheart took another step into the shed and shined his flashlight directly in my eyes. "Put your hands up."

I was not about to put my hands up like some common criminal. "Look, Detective Lockheart..."

"Put your hands up where I can see them."

"I think I know who did it."

"Ms. Michaels. I will not say it again, put your hands above your head."

I watched Detective Lockheart's outline as he pulled handcuffs out from his belt. That's when I realized he was actually going to handcuff me. He was going to arrest me.

"You can't be serious."

Detective Lockheart took two steps closer to me "I've never been more serious in my life. You are under arrest."

"You can't arrest me. I'm so close to finding proof."

"I told you that if I saw you anywhere near anything regarding this investigation, I would arrest you. Not to mention, you're breaking and entering, which is illegal. You refused to listen to me and now you're paying the price."

"You're telling me that I have to listen to you?"

"Yes, you do. For your own good, obviously."

"For my own good? Where do you get off?" I pulled my hand away when he tried to take my wrist behind my back. I spun around to face him, keeping my weight firmly on my good leg.

I stared for an uncomfortable moment into his eyes. He looked away. "You do not want me to add resisting arrest to the report."

"There shouldn't be any report except that I'm helping you solve this crime."

"The only thing you're doing is getting in the way of my investigation."

"So, you arrest me?"

"You refused to follow my instruction, which was not to get involved." He articulated those last words like I was a child. This lit a fire under me that I could not explain. I yanked my other hand free and marched out of the shed.

He was behind me before I even realized it, he grabbed my right wrist abruptly, which smarted, and I heard the click of the handcuffs. He didn't rush to grab my left wrist. He simply stood there and waited until I handed it to him, and he clicked the second handcuffed closed. I yanked hard against the handcuffs which he held with one hand as he turned off his flashlight and pulled the shed door closed.

BOOKING WAS AN INTERESTING EXPERIENCE. I hadn't known that they did digital fingerprints these days.

"At least I won't mess up my mani," I said to the processing cop.

She didn't smile. I didn't see Detective Lockheart again. I suppose he was busy filling out paperwork. I was still angry enough to think that I didn't care if he put resisting arrest in there. But after a few moments of calm reflection, I hoped he wouldn't.

The processing cop took me down to the basement where the wonderful cell was located. She escorted me in and turned around and closed the gate with a resounding bang. After she left, I looked around the room. "Well, here's the small room you talked about, Darla." I realized I still had my cell phone in my back pocket. Weren't they supposed to take that from me? Well, I certainly wasn't about to remind them. I pulled it out and looked. Yep, it had been my sister. I exhaled heavily. She had known seconds before I was arrested that I was about to be arrested. I shook my head. Life with a psychic sister. I wasn't about to text her back and let her know how right she was.

I looked at the time. 11:45 p.m.. It was probably too late to text Aerie. I jammed the phone back into my pocket. I didn't want her posting the bail or whatever it was that had to get done in order for me to get out of here, anyway. She didn't have the money. Ha. Neither did I. My ankle was tender. I limped over to the cot. The whole room smelled strongly of disinfectant. I sat tentatively on the edge. Ugh, would I really have to sleep here tonight? I glanced at the pillow. It seemed clean enough. I laid back on the cot and closed my eyes. Each time I breathed in, I felt the pulse of my ankle. I fell asleep.

16

I woke up the next morning with a stiff neck and an aching ankle. It took me a moment to realize where I was. The stupid jail cell. My anger for Detective Lockheart compounded tenfold.

And then I thought of Arnold and Ozzy and her morning walk.

I texted Aerie. *Can you please take Ozzy for a walk? I'm not home.*

Where the heck are you?

You don't want to know.

You got arrested last night, didn't you?

I waited a moment before I texted back because I didn't actually want to admit it. *Yes.*

I'll walk Ozzy and feed Arnold. No worries. But you have to tell me what's going on.

I texted her the details and explained that I had been in the maintenance shed looking for evidence against Terry for the crime. But Detective Lockheart had caught me before I found anything.

After thinking for a moment, I knew what she needed to do.

He's planning on poisoning Gerard again. It only made sense. In his mind Gerard was the last thing standing in his way to Nancy. There had to be more poisoned Lifesavers somewhere.

I need you to go to the municipal building and somehow get to wherever Terry works, his desk or office, whatever and search the place.

17

Aerie had managed to get Chelsea to meet her at the diner by telling a white lie that Jay was waiting for her in the parking lot. After some indignant screaming on both sides, Aerie finally said the one word she was avoiding. "Please?"

"Tell me again why I should help you?" Chelsea had her hands on her hips in that authoritarian way she always had.

Aerie suddenly understood why Mira couldn't help herself around Detective Lockheart. Because she was having a severely hard time managing not to throw something at Chelsea.

"You don't have to help. And maybe you shouldn't. But don't you think this will earn you brownie points with Jay?"

"Fine. What do we need to do?"

"We need to visit Terry Walburn's desk in the municipal building."

"You need me. You need my access code to the front door."

"You have it, right? Don't you drop paperwork off after hours?"

"I do. I don't like the idea of helping you or Mira. The only thing you guys have done for me is make my life harder."

Aerie felt like throttling her. Did Chelsea not remember bullying Aerie incessantly throughout middle school?

"Mira believes that Detective Lockheart is zeroed in on Nancy Walburn as the murderer because she has a strong motive. But Mira is pretty sure it was Terry."

"What makes her the queen of knowing?"

"She's done all of the investigating. "

"Why doesn't she keep investigating if she is so important?"

"Detective Lockheart has her in jail."

At this Chelsea burst out laughing. "Oh, that's good. Can I get a photo? Tell her to do a selfie. Make sure the bars are in the background."

"Are you done? Look, I'm telling you, if you help us with this, it will make Jay really thankful. Because that means the diner will get back to its regular business. You don't think he relies on that money?"

Chelsea sobered at that. "Okay, fine. When are we going to do this?"

"Right now." Aerie pulled her keys out of her pocket. If she had to partner with Chelsea at least she would be the one driving.

18

The booking officer came down and opened the door. "You're free to go."

"That's it?" I had expected to have a trial or something where I'd need a lawyer.

"Detective Lockheart said it was a warning."

I nodded skeptically. "I see."

I stuffed my phone in my pocket and left the small cell behind. But once I got upstairs to the active area of the station things were going crazy.

I heard Nancy's voice first. "I haven't done anything."

"She wouldn't poison me of all people." A voice that I assumed was Gerard's.

When I reached the top of the stairs, I saw Detective Lockheart glaring at Gerard. "She has plenty of motive. And we need to sit down and talk."

"She's not talking to you without a lawyer!" he shouted and turned to Nancy. "Honey, don't say anything until I get one."

Nancy nodded. Tears streamed down her face.

I marched up to Detective Lockheart. Well, as much marching as I could do with a sore ankle. "She didn't do it." Detective Lockheart turned to me. "I thought a night in jail would teach you not to meddle in police affairs. If you need another night, I'm more than happy to make that happen."

I caught Nancy's attention. "I know you didn't do this, Nancy. We've almost got it figured out. I promise."

"What are you talking about?" Detective Lockheart snapped.

"I know who committed the murders and we should have the evidence you need to book him."

The detective waved his finger in my face. "Do not, under any circumstances, do anything of the sort."

Chelsea and Aerie pushed through the front doors of the police station. Chelsea waved her cell phone in front of her. "We've got it."

"Got what?" Detective Lockheart bellowed.

"Evidence," Aerie added.

Chelsea invaded Detective Lockheart's personal space like it was her duty and pushed her cell phone into his hands.

"We have photos of the other poisoned Lifesavers in Terry Walburn's office at the municipal building," Chelsea announced triumphantly.

Dan Lockheart looked at me, disbelieving. "I lock you up and you send these two to break into the municipal building? "

Chelsea tugged his arm. "No, no. I had access. For my job."

Dan looked at the photos. "These aren't admissible in court if you obtained them illegally. And since you aren't the police with a warrant and had no right to be there, this evidence was obtained illegally. That means I can't prosecute Terry Walburn."

We looked at Detective Lockheart in disbelief. This all was for nothing? My ankle suddenly throbbed and I dropped into a nearby chair.

Terry Walburn burst into the police station like a tornado. "Where is she? Where's Nancy?" His eyes locked on her and he made a beeline for the group of us. Gerard stepped in the way and put a hand on Terry's chest. "Where do you think you're going?"

"To see my…Nancy. What is going on?"

Detective Lockheart stepped in. "This is not a circus. Everyone out. There is procedure and we will follow it." He nodded to a few officers lounging nearby. "Please escort everyone out, starting with Terry." The officers grabbed Terry and hauled him to the door.

"Wait." I stood, favoring my weak leg.

I glanced at Detective Lockheart as I moved the few feet between me and Terry. I thought I saw a look of concern in Dan's eyes before they hardened into the look he always gave me when I was about to interfere. I glared, hoping he would give me leeway for once.

"Terry, Nancy is being arrested for the murder of her husband."

Terry wrestled out of the officers' arms until he was facing me. "No!"

Out of the corner of my eyes, I saw Dan gesture to the officers to stand down. But he also stood at the ready.

"You don't want Nancy to spend her life in jail for this, do you?"

"Nancy…" Terry took a step toward her. He shook his head.

Nancy stumbled back. All the color had drained from her face and she seemed unsteady. Dan guided her gently to a nearby chair.

I focused back on Terry. "Nobody can protect Nancy now--she's going to go to jail for murder." I shook my head at Terry.

His face changed from panic to determination. "I can protect Nancy. I can protect her."

I felt like all he needed was one more nudge. "But how can you do that when she goes to jail?"

"I did it. I got rid of Eddie."

At Dan's nod, one of the officers handcuffed Terry. As he walked past us, he fell at Nancy's feet. "I love you, Nancy." An officer pulled him to his feet again and pushed him toward the steps down to the cell I had just vacated.

"For you, Nancy. Only for you." His voice pierced the silence. Nancy's hand flew to her mouth and she choked back a sob.

"Nancy, you're free to go. Mira, you're going to get yourself in trouble if you keep meddling with murder investigations." Dan sat down hard into his desk and pulled out a form.

"Is that an order, Detective Lockheart, to stop investigating?"

"It's a prediction. And one I'm having a problem with it coming true."

Aerie flashed me a look, one I wasn't sure I wanted to decipher. I flashed her one back. As if I was going to let it go that she and Chelsea had worked together to get us the evidence we needed to solve the case.

I beamed as I left the station, only limping a little. "We did it. Great job you guys. A murderer's confession in the middle of the packed police station." We were getting good at this. No matter what the detective said. There was only one thing left to do. After all, he wasn't the only one who was making predictions in my life.

"You guys go ahead; I have a phone call to make."

19

Once the town learned that Terry had been arrested, people started coming back to the diner. Breakfast the next day wasn't a rush but that was fine by me and my ankle. We had decided not to serve soup for the time being. Also, another thing I was okay with.

After the morning hours on my feet, I hobbled to the closest stool at the counter. My ankle was still tender, but I refused to use the crutches. My armpits needed the break.

"My sister says 'hi.'," I told Aerie. "She wants to meet you someday."

She grinned. "And?"

I grinned back. "Well, some things never change. But she was very grateful to hear from me and I was grateful to be able to tell her that everything was now fine."

"And?"

"I let her know that her premonition was right. I was stuck in a room. I didn't tell her it was a cell at the local police station, and she knows I'm holding back. But that's fine. I need her to trust me to get myself out of the scrapes I get myself into. I asked her to let me live my life here without too much intervention."

"Too much intervention?"

"She refused to promise she would never call me if she had a premonition about anything."

"It could be a good thing."

"We'll see," I said skeptically. "How are things with Jay?"

She pinched her lips together and nodded. "Better. I still wish he wasn't dating Chelsea, but better."

"The way you two flew into the police station together, I thought for a minute, maybe *you* were dating Chelsea."

Aerie let out a laugh. "I wouldn't go that far. We worked together to help you and Jay. It wasn't nearly as bad as I thought it would be. My brother is going to stay at Chelsea's for a while, but he said he'd come by and hang out here more often."

"Good. It'll be nice to see him around the diner."

"And around your little construction site?"

"Yeah, that too." I was getting tired of having a hole in my house. "Do you think he'll come back and help finish the kitchen?"

Aerie grinned and pulled me by the elbow toward the front of the diner. "He wanted to surprise you."

"What?" Confused, I looked out the window and I could see someone on my front porch. Jay was laying out a length of chain and looping it around a hook in the porch ceiling. "What is he doing exactly?"

"Hanging a new porch swing for you." She grinned. "He said he was renovating a house a few months back and they got rid of the swing, but Jay kept it. Our porch is too small and he figured he owed you for clearing the diner."

"You guys do so much for me as it is."

"That's what friends are for."

I turned and gave Aerie a quick hug. "Thanks for everything."

"Ditto."

"Speaking of dating..." Aerie grinned at me and her non-sequitur. "What do you think about Sam?"

"I think we should grab a bottle of sparkling cider and talk about him over dessert at my house."

Just then the bell on the door chimed. An unexpected customer had arrived. Only it didn't appear to either of us that Nancy would be a customer, at least not today. She wheeled in a very large cage. Inside the cage perched the scarlet macaw we had seen at the newspaper office. Nancy looked disheveled but relieved.

"Can we get you something to drink?" Aerie asked.

She laughed at the request. "No. But thank you." Nancy turned to me. "Mira, they told me at the newspaper that you really like Taco. I'd like to give him to you."

"What?"

"It was Ed's bird, and, well, I can't keep him. And they don't want him down at the newspaper, supposedly he was messing with their phone messages or something."

She pushed the birdcage in my direction. I shook my head. "I don't think I could..."

"He's better off with you than me." She gave the bird a dark look. "I'd probably kill him." She pivoted to me. "Inadvertently, of course." She turned to leave.

I stammered. What was going on?

When the diner door closed. Reality hit me. The bird was mine. "What just happened?" I looked at Aerie for some sort of reality check.

"I think you are the proud owner of Taco here."

The macaw shifted sideways on his perch and squawked so loud my ears rang. "Taco wants a beer; Taco wants a beer."

I looked to Aerie. Her shocked facade cracked. I almost fell off my stool. We laughed until we cried.

SNEAK PEEK OF CONSTRUCTION AND CALAMITY

The dark gray Ford 150 truck was parked in front of my house. My phone said 3:00 p.m., and Jay was already working on the construction of the kitchen. I opened my front door and stepped inside. My little pup Ozzy and the all-knowing Arnold greeted me at the door with yips and kitty rubs at my ankles. Taco squawked in the corner to get my attention.

"Hey Taco, how's it going."

"Hubba, hubba." I shook my head. He only 'hubba hubba-ed' when he saw me or Aerie, never for Jay or Sam or Dan. My sexist birdy was a new addition to my crazy family of foster pets. Finding a new home for a scarlet macaw with Taco's *skillset* was a tough prospect.

Ozzy barked and panted, excited that I was home. I scratched her behind the ears and rubbed her belly. I stroked Arnold's long black fur but cut the neck rub short.

Hey, I think you just shorted me the extra scratches.

"Extra scratches only happen when I don't get a bill for the vet in Philly.

Ah, my kittens.

"Yes. Exactly." I gave him treats anyway because he was Arnold. The kitten countdown had begun, and we were 3 weeks away from becoming kitten parents.

I sighed. First things first. The kitchen renovation.

Usually Jay would come by when his job was finished for the day. I was grateful for whatever time he could put in. It wasn't so long ago that he had refused to set foot in my house because we were arguing over whether his girlfriend, Chelsea, had poisoned a Soup and Scoop customer.

Aerie, Jay's sister, and I thoroughly believed it, mostly because of her past experience being Aerie's school bully. But things changed once she helped us find the true killer, and we're all learning to get along, mostly.

Today, the diner had been especially busy. After almost two weeks of a handful of customers, due to the aforementioned murder/poisoning at the diner, it was a welcome relief to be so busy that we didn't even notice the passing of time. All of a sudden it was 2:30 and closing time.

I still hadn't added soup back to the menu. Which was saying a lot for a diner named the Soup and Scoop. I had been focusing more on the "Scoop" aspect and new ice cream ideas.

As much as I wanted to get off my feet, I greeted the animals and went back outside to see how the kitchen was coming along.

I pulled my disheveled ponytail out and shook my hair loose to my shoulders. I still had a bit of a crush on Jay, even if I didn't want to admit it.

I turned the corner from the front of the house to the side yard where the kitchen protruded like a fresh framed box. "Hey there. How's it going?" I shouted over the sound of the nail gun.

Jay stepped out from behind the framed wall, shirtless.

My breath caught in my throat. Crush magnified. I let out the air stuck in my throat and sighed. "How's it going?" I attempted not to ogle by putting on a friendly smile.

His grin at me made it worse. I took another deep breath.

"It's great. The kitchen is framed out and ready for drywall. Do you know what kind of cabinets you'll want?"

Nope, not at all actually, but I told him, "I'm still thinking it over."

The idea of purchasing all the cabinets in one go made my savings account weep silently. And then there were the appliances. I got dizzy just thinking about it.

A wave of concern swept over Jay's features, "You okay?" he quickly put down the nail gun, ready to catch me.

I shook myself and laughed it off. "Yeah, yeah. Just tired from working at the diner."

His grin returned. "Business is back?"

"And then some. I think Mrs. Orsa brought the entire historical society in for breakfast today."

"Ha. I'll try to bring the guys from the site over for lunch tomorrow."

"Where are you working this week?"

"Over at Miller's Barn. He needs a new shed. Actually, it's an extra-large chicken coop."

"Really? So, I guess you guys aren't using the crane I saw driving down Main yesterday?"

"That would be for the theater going in at the Spring Creek Plaza. An old friend of mine is the general contractor over there."

"Are they almost done?"

"I think so; they're hanging the signage today."

There was an awkward silence, and we both stood staring at our feet.

"How's the kitchen coming? You mentioned dry wall?" I asked, walking over and picking a dandelion out of the lawn. "I had to chase some squirrels out of here the other morning."

He bent down and picked up his t-shirt and shook it out. "Yep." He pulled the t-shirt over his head. "I just need to get one of my guys to come with me to pick it up and we can have it installed pretty quickly. About half a day or so. Not long."

"Wow, I might actually have walls again."

"Yeah, I can pull out that plywood board between the rest of the house and you won't have to come out here see your kitchen or worry about squirrels."

"I'd make some joke about this would force me to cook, but you know..." He knew I cooked all morning at his sister's diner. He owned a stake in the diner too, he just never mentioned it.

"Well, you'll now be able to relax in a sunny kitchen sipping your coffee before you come to the diner."

"That would be nice. I can't thank you enough for helping out with this Jay."

"Oh, no problem, really. It feels good to do something for someone. And like I feel bad about Chelsea..."

He didn't have to spell out that he felt bad about Chelsea connecting her right hook to my left cheek a few weeks back. She had barely hit me, "It's all water under the bridge."

"Yeah? I hope so."

"Even Aerie is warming up to her; the other day she offered her a blueberry muffin on the house."

Jay chuckled, "Chelsea came home and said it confused her, she wasn't sure if Aerie was being nice or if she should accuse her of wanting her to gain weight."

"Sounds about right. Hey, do you want a soda?"

"Nah, I'll finish up here and head out. I'm taking Chelsea out for her birthday."

A pang of regret hit me in the pit of my stomach that made me mad. I was supposed to be over this stupid crush. I forced a smile on my lips. "Where are you guys going to go?"

"I wanted to take her somewhere in the city, something nice, so we're going over to Linguini's. It's an Italian restaurant near the capitol building."

"That should be nice." I needed to get away, just to gain my sanity. "Well, I'll let you get back to work. Thanks again, Jay."

"Yeah, no problem." He disappeared back into the frame of the kitchen where I could hear him put the nail gun back to use as I made my way to the front of the house. Jay was pretty much occupied by Chelsea. So even though he was the most generous and sweet, not to mention handsome, guy I knew in town, I would have to let that crush go and focus on a decent level of friendship status.

My stomach rumbled. Maybe I'd ask Aerie if she'd want to head over to the Pizza Pub for dinner tonight. I had a feeling she'd say yes, even if she wasn't hungry for pizza. Sam, the owner of the Pizza Pub, had been by the diner a few times this week just to chat with Aerie. My guess was she'd be more than happy to get pizza with me tonight. Maybe I wouldn't be having a date at Linguini's anytime soon, but I had a feeling Aerie might, if she played her cards right. And I, as her best friend, was here to help.

ONCE IN MY CAR, Babs, the Buick, had been kind enough to start, I filled her in on my chat with Jay. "I hear that Jay is taking Chelsea to Linguini's tonight."

"Is that right?" She tightened her blond ponytail. She was pretending not to care.

"He didn't tell you?"

"No. But I think he still believes that I will react badly."

"Like that hasn't happened in the past." I suppressed a laugh.

"Well, I'm over it. I've been meditating on this and I've come to terms with the fact that Jay lo... likes Chelsea. And that they are together. My brother has his own life." All the words came out of her mouth like she was reciting from memory.

"I think I hear your teeth grinding."

"Oh, please. It's hard enough. I still can't stand her. And she can't stand me, so it's even-ground."

"Just call me when there's a catfight," I said.

"You know she would be the one to start it."

"And you would finish it."

"You've got that right."

I snorted through my nose. I had no doubt that Aerie could hold her own. She rarely got angry but when she did, oh boy.

I wanted to change the subject to something more appealing than Chelsea and Jay's relationship. "So, Sam has been by the diner quite a bit lately."

"Oh, I hadn't noticed." She grinned to herself.

"You can't be coy with me. How is it going?"

"He's very nice."

"Nice? That's all I get? Come on, spill it."

"He is very sweet. And I like him." I glanced over and the smile was still there.

"This is why I knew I could talk you into having pizza tonight for dinner."

"Yes, maybe and also because Sam has started to carry vegan cheese for his pizzas."

"A suggestion from his new "girlfriend"?" I prodded.

"We're not boyfriend and girlfriend, yet."

I nodded. "Yet is the operative term. I see you guys together by the end of the week."

"I wouldn't have any objections about that."

"Sweet. The game is on. I will have him asking you out by next Friday."

She shifted quickly in her car seat to look at me. "No, no. Don't mess anything up. I don't want you to push him into it. I want it to happen naturally."

"You sound like a laxative ad."

"I do not. You just leave him alone. I can make sure we end up on a date by next Friday."

"I have no doubt." I smiled. Once Aerie set her mind to something, she made it happen.

I pulled into the Pizza Pub expecting to find the crane hovering over the newly built theater addition to the Plaza, but there were only a few pickup trucks and cars in the lot.

The sign wasn't up either. It sat crookedly next to the entrance of the theater. Yellow caution tape was still tacked to the cones across the sidewalk, prohibiting entry to the work site. The Pizza Pub's entrance was right next to the construction. Sam had been thrilled when he got the approval to open his wall into the theater entrance. Late-night moviegoers equaled lots of pizza orders.

I opened the door and the intoxicating scent of the pizza ovens engulfed us. "Hello, my favorite ladies!" Sam announced as we entered.

Aerie practically beamed like sunshine.

"Hey, Sam. I talked Aerie into coming over for dinner tonight. She said you had some new vegan cheese you are trying out?"

"Yes, I do. Would you like some on your pizza, Mira?"

"Ah, no. I'm not there yet."

"Got it. What can I get you ladies?"

Aerie leaned slightly into the counter never taking her eyes off Sam's. "Can I get a small gluten-free, vegan with mushroom?" I had never seen Aerie so smitten. It was adorable.

"Absolutely, my dear." Sam turned to me. "And what can I get for you?"

"Can I get a large, regular cheese, with onions and peppers?" I asked.

"Will do. I should have these up in 20 minutes, ladies. Please have a seat." He waved an inviting hand around the dining area. "Any one you want."

Aerie and I chose the booth closest to the counter. Aerie, of course, chose to sit on the side facing Sam, and I sat facing the entrance.

Detective Lockheart walked in through the door. I pushed myself as tightly as possible into the corner of the booth. I whispered, "Don't turn around, Detective Lockheart just came in."

"What, Dan?" Aerie turned in her seat to look and the detective caught the movement and saw me.

"Why am I not surprised?" He said with an exasperated look on his face. He practically rolled his eyes.

"I'm allowed to have dinner, aren't I?" I straightened in the booth.

"No. Not when it's at a crime scene."

At those words Sam perked up and walked back to the counter. "What's this about? A crime scene?"

"Hey, Sam. I'm just here to ask a few questions about the theft that occurred at the work site this morning."

"This is the first I've heard of it." He dusted off his hands.

"Yeah, I got the call early this morning from the general contractor. It seems the crane has been removed from the property."

"The crane? That's impressive."

"It's theft. Anyway, I need to ask you a few questions. Did you see anything suspicious last evening?"

Sam stood there a moment thinking. "The crew comes in and eats here, mostly on their lunch break. But last night one of the guys came in for dinner."

Dan pulled out his notebook and scribbled with a pencil. "And who would that be?"

"The guy named Travis. He stayed late, had a lot of beers and I called him a cab."

"What time would you say you called the cab?"

"Hmm. Think it was about 9:30 p.m."

Dan scribbled in his note pad. "Is there anything else you can think of. Anything that was out of the ordinary?"

Sam took a moment and continued. "Yeah, I guess I was surprised Travis didn't have a truck parked out front. He was going to have to get a ride home whether he had been drinking or not."

Dan scribbled additional notes and closed his notebook, pushing the pencil into the wire coil and shoving the entire thing into his back pocket.

"Thanks, Sam. I appreciate your time." He reached out a hand and Sam shook it. Forgetting that he had a hand covered in flour. The detective shook off the flour and Sam handed him a few napkins.

"Sorry about that."

"Not a problem. You have a good evening Sam." As

Detective Lockheart walked out, he stopped mid-stride in front of our table. "And you." He pointed a finger at me. Something I hated. "No. That's all I have to say."

I was already fuming. And yet I couldn't come up with any kind of witty retort. He made me that mad. Aerie patted my arm and smiled. I looked at her. "What are you smiling at? He's such a jerk."

She nodded and smiled. "Yep." She said without any conviction.

A few moments later Sam walked over with our pizzas. With great flourish, he set them down at our table. He even handed both of us cloth napkins. I grinned to myself. Another influence from his soon to be girlfriend.

MORE MIRA MICHAELS MYSTERIES

If you enjoyed this story and would like to read more about Mira and her lovable cat Arnold, check out more of the Mira Michaels Mysteries.

Construction and Calamity
Carnival and Corpses
Pottery and Perps

Please consider writing a review on Amazon to let others know more about Mira's adventures, please don't share spoilers! Reviews help readers find these stories which helps writers like me. That way I can continue to write what I love and create more stories for you.

Thanks bunches,

Julia

SUBSCRIBE AND SAVE!

Simply go to Julia's website at www.juliakoty.com and click the subscribe button. You'll be included in our exclusive club and be the first to learn about new releases and special deals on the stories you love.

ABOUT THE AUTHOR

Julia Koty is a new author of cozy mysteries.

Julia spent her early childhood in a small town in Pennsylvania very similar to Pleasant Pond. Her house, also an old Victorian which her dad renovated, was indeed haunted.

Visit her website and subscribe to her newsletter to be a part of the group and learn about exclusive deals on upcoming books in the series.

 facebook.com/JuliaKotyAuthor